Something Very Human

Something Very Human

Hannah Retallick

Bridge House

British Library Cataloguing in Publication Data
A Record of this Publication is available from the British
Library

ISBN 978-1-914199-76-9

This edition published 2024 by Bridge House Publishing
Manchester, England

Cover illustration © Jonathan Retallick

Contents

A Long Line of Plastic Straws 9

Naughty Step 15

Clara By Every Name 17

dashed 24

Right Now 26

Becoming Lavender 36

Unspoken, Unheard 42

Those Nice Suits 46

Kiss My Stretchmarks and Call Me Tiger 52

When the Tour Guide Still Smiles 55

Native 61

Wayne's Name 65

Chanel No.5 on a Musty Woollen Coat 73

Half Dead but Whole Hilarious 75

When Seagulls 77

The Ones I Never Sent 87

Burning Me, Maybe 104

She Went There for the Weekend 106

Reflections of a Mature Woman Who Took an Unfortunate Tumble 114

Seven Ages of Lone 120

A Little Guidance about Precious Items Displayed Meaningfully 127

As She Lay in That Green Dress from M&S.................131

Dear Margaret, Love Fred................................136

They Didn't See Him.....................................139

Three Pairs of Bed Socks and Two Hot Water Bottles..141

That Organ is Mine.....................................148

The Word Has It..154

Golden Hair..157

I Resolve to Die at Sixty-five........................159

To Live..164

If the World Were Ending..............................173

Credits..176

About the Author......................................180

A Long Line of Plastic Straws

Carter, a nine-year-old who had recently moved to 4 Woodland Road, compensated for everything by trying to connect the longest line of plastic straws in the world. The obsession started at McDonald's, where his grandma took him every Saturday. She sat Carter down at a booth while she queued for the Happy Meal. It was a box of food and a boring toy; what was Happy about that? He did like his frosty chocolate milkshake, but not as much as the paper-covered straws. He blew the wrappers across the room. Grandma couldn't ask Carter to pick them up, so she did it herself and tottered to the bin. Carter scrunched one end of a straw and inserted it into the other.

He started the project in the garage, which smelled like cardboard and dust, on a long folding table; judging by its rickety groaning joints, it had been unloved since Grandpa died. On a hot day there was even a lingering hint of his musky aftershave.

Each week, Carter picked up more and more straws, grabbing them from the McDonald's dispenser while Grandma Chrissie supported his arm. She never told him to stop stuffing them into his hoodie pouch.

Their house was the first of a three-house terrace, right at the edge of the village. Their garden was overgrown now Grandpa wasn't there and had a low-lying fence separating them from the neighbour. The garage soon became too small for Carter's venture; he asked Grandma Chrissie to help by taking the straws outside.

Carter tucked his good leg underneath him and stretched the other out. He missed being able to feel his foot and sometimes woke at night, thinking he still could, but then he remembered. Working in the garden, it was too easy for his mind to wander. He tried to focus on other things, like the dampness of the grass and the rustling sound from a hedge, which was trimmed neatly on the neighbour's side.

'Quite a project you have there,' his grandma said, shielding her eyes from the stark cloud-filtered light.

And then she returned to the house. She hardly left it, apart from to check on Carter. She didn't do her own food shopping now; what was the point when the Tesco delivery service was so obliging? Carter had to ask what obliging meant. She said, 'Obliging is when people make things good for you.'

He glanced at the house. His grandmother was obliging, and calm. She never talked about any of it.

'Hello,' came a voice.

Carter jumped. The voice came from the next garden, the direction of the sun. All he could see through looking at the light was a shadow above the neighbour's fence and the red specks and dark patches in his own eyes.

'Hello?' Once Carter had shielded his eyes with his hand, he could see a boy about his age who was leaning on the fence, making it creak and groan.

'What are you doing?' the boy asked.

He felt silly when he told him. 'I'm… I'm making the longest line of plastic straws in the world.'

But Billy didn't seem to think it was silly. 'Cool. How long does that have to be?'

'Erm, long. Really long.'

'Why don't you do it underground?' Billy suggested.

Carter bristled. 'I can't, it's plastic. That's bad for the earth.'

Billy climbed over the fence, landed softly, and darted over to where Carter sat. He joined him, mirroring his position, with one leg stretched out in front and the other tucked under him.

'What happened to your foot?' Billy asked, in the matter-of-fact voice that no one else used with Carter. 'I've seen you...'

'It was trapped in the car.' Carter touched one of his crutches.

'Okay...' Billy nodded slowly. 'You know, my mum has a big box of straws in the cupboard for when we have parties. I could ask her?'

Billy's mum was a nice lady called Tara. She smelled like roses and felt soft and plump when she hugged him, which she did as soon as Billy made the introduction at the doorway of their house. Carter's own mother had always been a hugger too and helped him with his homework and took him to play football at the Green, back when he had two proper feet to use and... but he didn't have to worry about that at the moment because the adults decided he should have time to 'process everything'.

Tara was happy to help and presented a box of straws that were a mixture of colours, to make a change from the white ones with thin coloured lines.

'Actually,' said Carter, holding the box of straws. 'I think I'll stick with the McDonald's ones.'

Billy's mother just smiled and told them to have fun.

Billy helped Carter connect the straws. It was not long before the line stretched over Carter's whole garden and under the fence. Tara provided cans of Fanta and Grandma came to say hello, perhaps checking if Billy was 'suitable company'.

'Where are your parents?' asked Billy, dragging a chipped terracotta pot to pin down a section.

'I'm living with Grandma.'

'Oh.'

'Where's your dad?' asked Carter.

'Mum says he scarpered when I was little.'

'What's scarpered?'

11

'Ran away cos he didn't want us.'

Carter tried to imagine what this would be like. 'Oh…'

'Yeah.'

Carter's dad hadn't 'scarpered'. He'd held his mum's hand and his whenever he could. Dad said it was to make sure no one got lost, but Carter didn't think that was it; he just liked them being connected.

The straw line progressed quickly; Billy's kind mother started taking Billy to McDonald's at the same time as Carter and his grandma, doubling the number of straws they were able to sneak out.

'We really shouldn't let them,' said Chrissie, on their second visit.

'No, we really shouldn't, should we…' Tara chomped into a Big Mac and put her hand under her chin to stop the trickle of sauce in its tracks.

The two women smiled at each other and said no more. They had never really talked before Carter came to stay, but now they often had a cuppa and chat together, initially over the garden fence. Then they started going inside, especially on rainy days. Grandma and Tara would sit downstairs while Carter and Billy played in each other's rooms – video games, mostly, though they also liked to construct big Lego towers. Yet their 'great big straw line', as Tara called it, was their favourite thing to do together. The plan had been going so well; they had nearly reached the other side of Billy's garden.

Then one Saturday, everything changed.

Carter knew something was wrong the moment he felt the straws at McDonald's; they were lighter, flimsier. He unwrapped one, slowly, put it into his Coke, and after only a few minutes, the straw began to soften and his heart thumped harder.

'Billy,' he whispered. 'Billy, look.'

He drew out the straw, which made a screeching sound as it left the claws of the plastic lid. It was limp and starting to break.

Carter's crutches swished through the overgrown grass until he was just a couple of feet from Billy's neighbour's fence. They had discussed only earlier that morning how they would knock on the old man's door, ask if he would let them carry on in his garden, but now it wasn't possible: McDonald's had changed their straws from plastic to paper.

'I guess that's it then,' said Billy.

'Yeah.'

'How did your foot get trapped in the car?' he asked, suddenly.

This time, Carter gave the real answer. His parents had told him many times not to squeeze his leg between the seat and the door.

'And then the lorry hit us. And then I woke up in hospital. And then...'

They would never tell him off again.

'Your parents died, didn't they?'

It was the first time Carter had cried about it; it was the first time anyone had said 'died'.

'And now my foot doesn't work. And I can't do the straws anymore because of stupid Maccies.'

Billy threw his arms around Carter. It knocked the crutches out of his hands, but with Billy gripping so hard, he didn't fall. Billy didn't smell of roses like his mother and wasn't soft; he was sticky and skinny.

'It's okay...' Billy didn't sound like he believed himself. 'At least the paper straws won't hurt the earth. You know?'

Carter nodded, banging his chin on Billy's bony

shoulder. He broke the hug, squatted to the floor on one leg, and wiped his nose, leaving a trail on his sleeve. 'I guess so.'

'It'll be okay.'

'You're obliging, Billy.'

They sat there, silently. Carter glanced towards the house and wondered what the adults were talking about – maybe Grandpa, the car accident, or Tara's man. Or maybe they were talking about plastic straws. All that potential.

'Billy,' said Carter.

'Yeah?'

'I've been thinking about towers.'

Naughty Step

I was put on the naughty step again. He told me if I moved something bad would happen. Bad things happen anyway.

Daddy's girlfriend comes here lots and I don't like her because she shouts at him sometimes and I have to pin my hands to my ears until she stops or else I cry and then Daddy shakes me and says not to be such a wimpy baby. Daddy doesn't even cry when he has big cuts bleeding on his face. I want to be brave like him when I grow up.

Her name is Jade. I don't know why he would want to see her when she screams and stamps and throws bottles at his head. That was the bad thing that happened today. Only one bottle hit him and the other smashed on the wall because he dodged out of the way and then he saw me spying and put me on the naughty step in the hall.

Jade went without saying anything to me as she passed. I leant forward and saw Daddy on the sofa with his head on his hands. He was there for ages and my bottom went fuzzy on the hard naughty step and then he came over to me.

'I'm going to Jade's.' He put his big puffy black coat on. 'I need to say sorry.'

'Why?'

'I made her cross somehow.'

'How?'

'Don't move a muscle, Isaac. I'll be back soon, okay?'

I don't like it when he leaves me on my own but always try to be brave and he's never gone too long.

As soon as the door slammed, I moved a muscle. I moved all my muscles. My legs stood me up and walked me into the living room and there was green glass and wetness on the carpet.

I didn't know what to do apart from wait for Daddy to get home. He always has a sound of love when he talks to her like she's better than ice cream with chocolate sauce and sprinkles. She looks pretty but isn't. Not like Mummy. I wish at least that the prettiness Mummy had inside her could be brought back to life and put into Jade's body and then maybe we could be nearly happy.

He should tell her to be nicer to him and not to throw things. It always goes quiet when they kiss on the mouth. Sometimes she says sorry, but it happens again, so I don't think she means it.

It's getting dark now and I'm scared because Daddy still isn't home. Maybe it's because I moved off the naughty step. *Something bad will happen.* If I sit back down again then maybe everything will be okay and Jade won't hurt Daddy anymore and he'll come back all safe.

I sit back down.

I say, 'Everything will be okay.'

It sounds shaky and it feels like a lie and I don't think I believe it anymore.

Clara By Every Name

My name is Clara and I'm not like other girls. I have been Janet, Gwendolyn, Katherine or Kathy, and every other name that my mother could form between a stranger's 'hello' and 'who's this lovely young lady then?' I answer to anything, with no more thought than if it were darlin' or hun. It's always been this way, ever since my mother saw the light, saw life for what it was, and withdrew. We travelled from place to place in her battered dark-blue van, foraged the hedgerows with nettle-stung hands and foraged the cities with her smiles, only spending money on essentials such as petrol, soap, paint, and black silk dresses.

We were in London for one cold winter, parked up on different side streets, never in the same place two nights running: too risky. No ID or driver's licence, but we would have been discovered in the end. *Found: middle-aged woman with young daughter, driving illegally. Help needed with identity. Is it… could it be them? The ones who disappeared all those years ago?* My mother was a professional shadow. The few times we were caught, her disguise held and she weaved her way out of trouble – I don't like to think about how; usually we weren't noticed at all. They had stopped looking. *Presumed dead?*

'Sweetie,' she'd say. 'If you look respectable, no one thinks to ask questions.'

I was nine years old and became Timothy, followed by Charlie, Michael, and Our Youngest Child Jeremy, but those were only during the weeks after the unfortunate 'professional' haircut, a backstreet job, £2 per child, a deal too glittery for my optimistic Father Figure to turn down. I was a boy, and I liked it at first, seeing how much more important it made me, how easily I could make my square jaw fit.

Its strength surged to my fists as I used them to show Bob Punter that I was indeed not like other girls. He was a boy a few years older than me who tried to take my cola-bottle sweets, thinking I was an easy victim, skinny and scraggy. I pushed him against a filthy dustbin and beat him around the head with our latest discarded number plate. His weeping cuts begged for mercy.

Then my blond mop grew back, curving around my chin. I felt myself shrink, weaken, but not completely disappear. And then a new strength. I was a girl by the time we moved on again and have been ever since.

When I was twelve, we drove west through Devon and along the north coast of Cornwall. Angelica. That was the name I was given during the spring that Father Figure asked my mother an unexpected question. She said she would, but he didn't last long after that. Some things are better left unsaid. When Mother had met him, he was a stiff black suit, and she rescued him from the disease of modern society. But he relapsed.

Angelica was a comfort to her then, with her powerful waves of empathy. Gentle and soft, nurturing, motherly, even as a twelve-year-old. I was Angelica for a long time to help her get over it, because she was heartbroken, you see, even though it was her decision – heartbroken that he wanted to stand still while she craved movement, that he wanted to be visible, burned into a lifelong contract, while she craved invisibility.

Mother took to sprawling on a big rock in a nameless cove – the same time every day, when and where he had asked – like a beached mermaid. It was the longest we were ever in a single place. She regretted that weakness but couldn't quite escape it.

On the last day we were there, she wore no coat even though it was a cold spring, and her skin was goose-bumped on her bare arms and upper chest. I returned to the van after a couple of hours of silent sitting. Using our camping stove, I warmed some sugary water, dipped in an overused teabag, and poured it into her red mug. As I crossed the rocks, trying to hold on to my notebook and the drink, I stumbled and sloshed tea into a shallow rock pool. I froze for a moment, transfixed by the cloud of milk that spread through the water and the ripples that eventually came to rest. How might that feel?

'Thank you, Jeremy. I mean, Angelica. Sorry,' said Mother. She took a lock of my growing fringe, sizing it up.

'Do you need anything else?' Angelica was a bit of a doormat really.

'You're writing?'

'Yes. I'm Charlotte, Mummy,' I said, daring to try a different name, even if it wasn't the one I wanted.

She looked through me, then back to the sea. 'I suppose you'd better get on with it then, hadn't you?'

My bare feet became cold on the rock as I waited for goodness knows what.

Soon enough, she started naming me again. For the following two years I was Anne, Emily, Jane, Virginia, and as we travelled through northern England and into North Wales, I became Collette. Mother liked her spunkiness. Feisty and rebellious, this girl helped her mother steal a silver notebook from a Tesco in Llandudno, tearing off the barcode.

'Never the small shops,' said Mother. 'They're our people.'

Father Figure used to say that too.

Mother and I cocooned in a forest in the mountains of Snowdonia. She cut my hair again but didn't make me a boy that time. I, Collette, perching on a fallen tree, wrote furiously with the fountain pen Mother abracadabraed into my life. Collette needed it, and BAM! There it was.

Is Mother a witch? Is she a thief, like Collette? A demon? Or an angel with special powers? A fairy? These were the sort of questions I wrote in my notebook, questions I didn't want to ask her directly. And then there was the matter I could never discuss and was almost too scared to write. It stirred an increasingly strong desire within me. I wrote the answer instead:

Clara.

The name was a possibility, a distant memory, a word chanted internally, a name given and then taken, because it didn't seem enough. I found myself wondering, not for the first time in my life, whether I really existed. Or if I do exist, whether I am sentenced to be either formulaic or formless.

These thoughts blew away one day. My notebook disappeared. I never asked where it went.

We returned to Cornwall when I was fifteen. She scanned everywhere we drove and parked, as though looking for something she'd lost there – an engagement ring, perhaps. We hadn't heard from him since. How could we?

'No phones, Cleo,' she said, wearily. 'Nothing they could use to track us.'

Was it tiredness in her voice, or was it grief, yearning for what she's given up?

Missing: white woman, 33 years old, long black hair, with a bemused baby. Concerned for whereabouts. Please come home, darling, etc.

We flowed onwards because the thing she's looking for is no longer here. I knew she missed Father Figure because she still muttered his name in her sleep: Andrew, Andrew, Andrew… Where is he? After all these years, where?

I remember watching her profile as we hurtled round corners on bendy roads and hedged lanes, trying to see through the webby mane she'd chopped above her jawline as if to punish herself. But all I could see was the tip of a damp nose that could no longer sniff out the right path for us. Her back was hunched, unable to hold itself. This mystical Tinker Bell was killing herself with a different kind of poison: her growing, repellent stubbornness. *I don't believe in fairies. I don't believe in fairies. I don't believe in fairies. I don't, I don't.* My stomach churned and I looked ahead; it didn't help, because it wasn't just travel sickness, was it?

These fragmented reflections plucked from my life are where they belong: not immortalised in a glittery notebook but scrawled on a scrap of paper that's as transient as I am.

It is winter now, the middle of January, and I have just turned sixteen. Chasing warmth, we returned to London. It will be her final resting place. Some things are inescapable.

Mother has told me her story at least once a year; as if I could forget. Picture this: a powerful woman fills a crisp white shirt and black pencil skirt. She nearly drowns in ninety-hour weeks, and when her head breaks the surface for a moment, she gasps for breath, not caring what's in the air and inhaling anyway. Nine months later, a problem enters the world. There are no longer ninety hours in a week to work. That's when she escaped.

Sixteen years later, here she is, sick, with lumps on her breasts and a seeping nipple. She won't go to the doctor because she still refuses to exist. Ms Smith, Ms Carmichael, Ms Jenkins… they have no passports or NHS numbers.

It is a frosty Sunday. I have driven us to a side street, which is illegal given my age and lack of licence, but then my whole life has been illegal really, hasn't it? I wrap the red knitted shawl around her – it's decorated with random holes, dropped stiches, and tragic tea stains. I perch on the edge of the narrow bed, its softness caving a little and tilting her sideways. I have become Ruth because she needs my care, a friend, a companion, not a daughter. I sleep curled up to her cold feet. She refuses all my food and drink offers, just shrinks. There's nothing more to say or do.

The most female thing that had ever walked the planet, everything that this world condemns and condones, is preparing for death in her classic black silk dress and the shawl of her making. If she had looked back to the beginning, she might have heard them say she'd had a breakdown and lost her mind. Alone, desperate and worked to the bone, she had been pulled left and right. They called for her whole being, every cell, every drop of blood. But what about me, The Problem? I screamed for her. I sucked my mother dry. My grandparents vampired her too. *You made your bed; you lie on it.*

The bed she has chosen now is a back-seat cradle. She's more trapped than ever, caught like a fish in an ice block. But she'll never change her mind, never admit that she's wrong, never give me what I need.

It's time.

I escape the claw fingers that plead with Janet, Gwendolyn, Katherine or Kathy, Ruth; with Timothy, Charlie, Michael, Our Youngest Child Jeremy; and with Charlotte, Anne, Emily, Jane, Virginia, Collette, Cleo and… Angelica.

'Angelica, please!' She's her last hope. 'Please, don't leave me.'

As I walk away and hear the cries from deep in her heaving chest, I imagine the message I would leave if we had phones: *I'm sorry, Mother, but Angelica cannot take your call. She doesn't exist. Beep.*

Instead, I turn, return to the open window next to her, and laser-scan her corpse-in-waiting.

'What do you want? Who are you calling?'

She can't or won't answer. I must leave. Given then

taken, just like my notebook, she stole my name from me, stole the life I could have had.

My name is Clara and I'm not like other girls. I *am* the other girls. All of them, in one body, not formless but fluid. They can't make me choose.

dashed

uncle peter said hed take me to the zoo on friday to see the tigers – we tried months ago when i was really little but the zoo people at the door said there was an accident in the elephant pen and it was shut that day sorry – even the tigers – when we got home uncle peter told mummy our hopes were dashed – he said next time it would be open and i could buy something from the giftshop and even have cake in the cafe if i was good and it wasn't too close to dinner time and how did that sound – it sounded very good

then he couldnt for ages and ages – he kept being too tired – i told him to sleep more – he must have listened to me because he got better and said fridays the day michelle – ill make sure he eats lots in the cafe – hes got skinny – ill have four pieces of chocolate cake to help him be squidgy again

i thought hopes could only get dashed one time – im always right mostly – now im wrong – they can get dashed two times – i know that because its happening

mummy says uncle peter cant go to the zoo on friday – she says hes gone to A Better Place – i wish hed taken me too – it must be very very good if its better than the zoo – mummy says we can go anyway but doesnt seem happy about it and starts crying and saying im sorry michelle im so so sorry – now shes snotting on her sleeve like she always tells me not to do – she knows how excited i was to go with uncle peter – now shes leaning on the table with her elbows like she always tells me not to do – i touch her arm – now shes shaking and feels like uncle peters shaver that i wasn't meant to use on my eyebrows – i told him he shouldnt have used it all over his head either and he said I was a cheeky little and then stopped

24

i think mummys upset because she really really doesnt want to be near the tigers – i tell her she shouldn't be scared because there are fences to keep people safe and if we don't climb over them we wont get hurt and make our hopes dashed – now shes crying more – i give her a bear hug and tell her its okay and she doesnt need to take me if she doesnt really want to – now her nose is dangling a snot tail so i pull lots of tissues out of the box for her before it can drop – she says thank you – it sounds like ank ooo—

its okay its okay i tell her lots of times – i can wait until uncle peter comes back from A Better Place if she doesnt want to go to the zoo – maybe hell be back by saturday

Right Now

I never shop here. The student loan isn't designed for this. People swerve past me as I stand at the entrance leaning on a trolley. Most of the customers look ordinary, with raincoats and weary expressions, but there's one guy in a tweed jacket, burgundy trousers and a flat cap who's so posh looking I want to laugh. I don't laugh. Em's dad might look like that. She would say I'm prejudiced and that you shouldn't judge someone until you know them.

She was excited about that Carl guy at first, with his black skinny jeans, easy handsomeness, and the flashy words falling from an otherwise empty head. He sauntered – yes, sauntered – into the living room and started poking around, with only a backwards nod to acknowledge me. He gave all these opinions while Em leaned against the bookcase, tilting like a cute ballerina, looking at him as if he were the best thing since macaroni cheese. Anyone can learn a few lines of the *Anna Karenina* wiki page, even me. I'm good with words, if they're in my head and don't have to be thought up on the spot or said out loud – thank goodness for English essays.

Carl, Carl, Carl. Seemed nice enough, is what I said when she asked me later. She always frowns when I say that, says it's a cop-out. It is. I don't know why she still asks.

Someone bumps my elbow and I venture into the fruit and veg aisle. I've no idea where anything is, or what I want to buy, so my chances of success range from minimal to non-existent. She says frozen veg is more nutritionally valuable; it's frozen only a couple of hours after picking, which means it retains more vitamins and minerals. She says go for frozen vegetables unless they're in season. I've never been good at remembering when things are in season, and I can't check – forgot my phone. It says 'British' on the broccoli's tightly wrapped packaging, but does that mean it's in season in this country or that they've been forced to grow in a hot house? Or do they grow in a mild climate? Or a cold climate? I know nothing. I need a lie down. The things I do for you, Em. It feels like an emergency though. Friends are always there for you in emergencies, even if 'there for you' involves a degrading supermarket experience.

I was in the kitchen when it first kicked off for Em, a couple of weeks back. I scooped a tin of Tesco's own brand baked beans into a saucepan – she says if you must eat those disgusting things, for goodness sake, please heat them up and use a plate or bowl or something. Friends, eh?

The door had opened and was slammed. Never a good sign. Did they know I was home? I hesitated too long to walk into the living room and say hello. I paused, with the tomato-covered wooden spoon suspended until a bit dripped on the counter. That was when the shouting started. He called her a bitch. A bitch? Really? I picked a stubborn bean from the edge of the tin and turned the hob on. Was she safe? I couldn't hear what she was saying – measured as ever, even in a crisis.

Food makes everything better – when you're eating it, I mean. When you're being a numpty in the supermarket, staring at 'sweet and tangy goats' cheese and caramelised onion ravioli'… not so much. It looks delicious, suitably posh but accessible for my common taste buds, and seems like the perfect option. I chuck it into my basket. And then I remember something she said about processed food, about how she didn't like to get anything that contained more than five ingredients because they put all sorts in there. Was it still bad if there were more than five luxury ingredients? I put the ravioli back on the shelf. It was probably too 'easy' anyway, and she would know I hadn't made it myself, Macaroni Cheese Boy.

We live above a small coffee shop. Our flat's the sort of place you can imagine the council might want to 'take a look at'. I don't know why Em's slumming it here. Something to do with proving herself, perhaps – proving her independence, proving she's not posh or privileged. Emily Smith: the girl who once ate my cold leftover Domino's pizza with a knife and fork!

A few days after it all kicked off, she hovered in the kitchen with her phone as I made myself some supper. Furious texting. I didn't say anything about Carl. If she'd wanted to talk about Carl, she would have talked about Carl, about why they had argued, about what had happened. They hadn't realised I'd heard anything, so I couldn't ask without giving myself away. I handed her a bowl full of macaroni cheese instead. She broke into a smile.

I reach the meat aisle, trolley still empty. I can't choose vegetables when I haven't decided on the main bit of the meal. I'm like a gormless child who's lost its mother, hanging around waiting to be found. If there's CCTV, what will they think? Speaking of shoplifting-prevention, there's a slab of meat wearing a sticker saying, 'Security Protected'! Does that mean one of those plastic things they have to take off at the till, like they have on clothes? Fair enough. This steak costs more than clothes – the ones I buy anyway.

Maybe how you like your steak is some indication of status. I have mine well done and Em has it rare. Raw. That cow could stand up and dance off the plate, as my mum would say. I have a feeling that beef is the best way to go. If it can be eaten raw, I won't give Em food poisoning if I cook it wrong. Beef it is.

I didn't expect her to accept that macaroni cheese, especially not when I'd chucked it in the bowl the wrong way up, the crispy topping invisible. She didn't even comment. I thought perhaps it was a distress signal, a cry for help, a sign that she had lost her mind, and I said as much. She laughed and said no, it's just exactly what I need right now, thanks James.

I shouldn't have felt flattered. It was the 'right now' of Pot Noodles and Ben and Jerry's and greasy KFC. The 'right now' of guess what that dickhead did? You remember, James, the one who was here the other day; tall, bit like James Franco if you're drunk and squint a bit? Carl – like I could forget. Yeah, that one. Dickhead. You share a name with his lookalike but nothing else, she added.

I shuffle along the ready-meal section. I may not be a food connoisseur, but this is where I draw a line. Anyone can chuck cheap tomato sauce on pre-cooked slimy pasta without the help of a snooty supermarket, with its wasteful plastic tubs and films to stab with a fork. They're three for the price of two though.

I'm glad she appreciated the food and that she complimented my addition of bacon and that it had given her comfort in the 'right now' caused by the dickhead that looked like James Franco. But when it comes to food, her 'right now' is one of my 'always'; macaroni cheese, creamy and comforting, eaten with cheerful friends in front of the tele.

I leave the ready meals on the shelf. I'm not here for cheap convenience. With beef in my basket – royal, sell-your-soul-to-pay-for-it beef – I feel a transformation coming. James, the man of taste and refinement, moves towards the fruit and veg with a spring in his step. Asparagus, wrapped in bacon, wrapped in plastic, catches my eye. She loves bacon, so this can't be a bad thing, can it? I check the packaging. You fry them. I like frying things; you can see when you've messed up.

Some people never accept when they've messed up,

think they can get away with anything if they make whiny enough apologies afterwards. Carl stooped down to her, squeezing her upper arms, begging. I sat on the sofa, head in a book, my eyes stuck on the first sentence of *Jane Eyre* – she'd said we couldn't be friends if I hadn't read it.

My peripheral vision scanned the unfolding drama. I'm so sorry, Emma, it won't happen again, I was stressed, work is bad right now and I lost it, I'm so sorry. Pah, about as sorry as a kid who's stolen his mum's chocolate. Look, said Em, you've got to stop doing this. I know, I know. That girl's no pushover. She gave him aggressively crossed arms, brown eyes flashing.

Anyway, vegetables. Parsnips? I pick up a bag of them and put it down again – think of the planet – choosing four loose parsnips instead, all knobbly and hairy with dirt in their crevices. Starchy they may be, Em, but they're the gods of root vegetables and are exactly what we need right now.

I'd eventually shut my book, breaking the invisible barrier between us. I made a cuppa for me and Em, briefly halting the fight, and offered one to Carl too. I'm not a dickhead. I scooped five teaspoons of sugar into her big red mug, the one that makes her hands look even daintier, and peeked around the doorframe to make sure he wasn't too close to her or getting angry again. I stirred her gloopy tea. The door slammed. When I returned, Carl had gone. She looked at me. I could see she expected me to say something. I didn't.

My heart flips when I reach the cookery section. A small, optimistic part of me thinks I can make her a special pudding, a cake or a tart or a crumble or a pie. When I'm faced with ten types of flour, I rethink. My efforts might make her smile and laugh, but not for the right reasons.

Once Em had done the necessary, she let go. She's a

pretty crier. Her face opens up rather than scrunching in, her eyes widening, holding shiny tears for a long time before blinking makes them fall. Beautiful. I shouldn't have thought this when she was in such distress. She's never down for long though. She's a survivor.

Billionaire's shortbread from the fridge. Shortbread and treacly caramel, topped with a thick layer of dark chocolate and sprinkled with flakes of… is that gold leaf? Sometimes millionaire's shortbread isn't enough. Em's parents are neither millionaires nor billionaires, unless they've inherited a fortune. Both are doctors. Doctors with high standards, who would rather their daughter was studying a 'proper subject' than sticking her head in fiction all day long – often romances too, goodness gracious me.

As always, Em was hopeful that the next guy would be better. It didn't take her long to find him. Mike. Seemed nice enough – I would happily describe him as a 'non-dickhead'. She'd scooped him up during a wander through the art department, complimenting his impressionistic canvas. (I made that up. Point is, he's an art student.) That guy did know what he was talking about – I didn't understand any of it. He's like her, only about paintings instead of books.

She likes inviting people for fancy meals, which seems old-fashioned and romantic. Always one-to-one, never dinner parties – not that there's room here. Old friends, new acquaintances… It's like she's testing them. Can you cope with Emily Smith and her ways? She manages to do things 'properly', even in the messy flat. We've piled books in corners, since the bookcases reached breaking point, and our little round table is squeezed in at the side of the living area. It's often our only clear surface.

On the evening with Mike, the table was neatly laid with cutlery and bright blue napkins, folded in a fan shape and placed on the white side plates – the candles only come out on special occasions. She's a strange fish, that's for sure. I apologised as I walked through and glimpsed her glazed-over face. I can tell when she's having to force her eyes to stay engaged. I retreated to my room, sat cross-legged on my bed, and listened to the rumble of Mike's voice. He was doing all the talking. She would be relieved when they reached the cheese board.

If only I could remember what they had. That orange one. Red Leicester? And something stinky. Danish Blue? And maybe a chewy cheese with red wax. Edam? I ate the casing when I was a kid – put me right off. Goats cheese, smoked cheese, cheesy cheese cheese… No, keep it simple. I won't put red grapes on the platter either. She'd laugh at me if I did that. One step too far. I wonder what Mr Art Student made of it. Seemed nice enough, I said, before she could ask.

She sat on the sofa, leg tucked under her, even though she knew it would go numb. Thing is, she said, frowning. I sat down beside her. Thing is, if I'm completely honest, I'd rather hang out with you than ever see him again. Is that weird?

I don't know, I said.

I don't mean it in a weird way, you know?

Yes.

The more I think about it, I'm like, James is so… nice!

What, James Franco?

Haha. There's no point even trying to compliment you.

Sorry. I meant 'thank you', Em.

That's better.

Aren't you meant to say 'you're welcome'?

You're welcome.

Thank you, I said.

You're welcome, she said.

That made us laugh.

I move towards the busy checkout, pulling up behind an old guy with a basket who's pushing his things onto the conveyor belt, one by one, tutting at the person ahead. The conveyor belt is full and piled high. That posh woman must have money falling out of her eye sockets. Her child, podgy and red-cheeked, is squeezed into the deep-trolley's seat, dressed in a navy-blue polka dot duffle coat, puffed out with the many layers that will protect her from the cold. She's screaming her heart out, nose streaming. Please, please stop, her mother says, throwing groceries into Bags for Life and a large wicker basket. Her heavy makeup seeps into the stress wrinkles on her forehead. Stop it, please stop it, she hisses, tears forming. She needs a hug so badly. *James is so… nice!*

Em slouched on the sofa, her head bent right back over its low top. Quiet, pale, worn down by life. I hadn't seen her like that before, not even after Carl. A real emergency. I sat beside her. We fell quiet.

Eventually, she turned to me, managing a weak smile. How about we have dinner tomorrow night? I was going to go out with Mike, but… Maybe we could go and eat someplace nice instead, or at home – so tired right now.

I'll cook, said my mouth. Oops. *James is so… nice!*

That would be lovely. She exhaled slowly. You always know how to make me feel better, James.

And this is how I come to be standing with a trolley full of foreign items by the checkout in Waitrose. Old guy with the basket is laying six bottles of wine on the belt. They roll back and forth. I've forgotten wine. I turn, and steer awkwardly around the person behind, who happily takes my place.

Wine is red or white or a mix of the two; that's all I know. I don't drink the stuff, being more of a cider guy myself. I peel the labels off her bottles, wash them, and put them in the recycling. Why have I never read the labels? I rub my forehead.

A middle-aged woman glances at me and my trolley. My ignorance had projected itself.

Go with Merlot, you can't go wrong, she says.

I pick it up and nod a thank you. There, we're done.

A member of staff tries to herd me to a newly opened checkout. I hang back, glimpsing a young woman sweeping towards the self-service checkout. She's so like Em. I thought it was her for a moment – the same energy, the same dyed deep-red hair.

Em's pale brown roots are starting to show now. She's not vain but takes pride in being 'well put together', always in miniskirts and thin black tights. She wears almost undetectable makeup. I see her without it every night. Even if she comes home late, tipsy, she swipes it with a face wipe, chatting merrily, and then does a 'deep cleanse' in the bathroom. She reappears, her pale face radiant and flushed from the scrubbing. Gorgeous. Then there's the leggings and the baggy grey hoody, the clothes no one would guess she owns, and the beaming smile as she tells me all about it. All about whatever.

You always know how to make me feel better, James.

The small round clock says 5:13. There's plenty of time.

I take a final trip around the supermarket, pushing the trolley that I only needed for support. It's much quicker in reverse, with no decisions to make, or food to ponder. I put it back; the beef, the asparagus wrapped in bacon wrapped in plastic, the parsnips, and the billionaire's shortbread. I keep the wine and linger in the cheese aisle. She once told me her dad uses parmesan – good flavour, more special – but she doesn't seem to mind either way on those 'right now' kind of days. In fact, she never seems to mind at all.

I exchange the Red Leicester, Danish Blue and Edam for two bags of grated cheddar, buy one get one half price, and whiz back to the meat section, chucking a packet of streaky bacon into the trolley. I have everything else. Maybe I'll make her some fancy food another time. Right now, I don't think that's what she needs.

Becoming Lavender

Act 1

I unlock the bungalow door and the smell hits me. Urine and lavender. I pause for a moment. Dear Granny, she was such a stinker. Lavender by name, Lavender by… scent. A walking predictability.

It isn't urine, it's mustiness. Old dusty lavender, hanging in the living room, and sitting in all the drawers no doubt. I dip my hand into my bag and pull out a small mango perfume, spraying it in my path.

Anyway, I've gone off script. I'm meant to be doing… what did Mum say? First, windows: get some air in. That's a high priority, or we'll never get a buyer. She's not wrong. Mum must sell the house, you see, and I agreed to go on ahead to sort things out.

This is the acting job of my life. Well, not really an acting job, but that's what I like to think. Reinvent myself, why not?

My name is Demelza and I belong to Cornwall.

In St Ives, they will see this, they will see me as I want to be. If I'm not too high on lavender, that is. Can you get high on lavender?

I'm surprised this smell didn't drive Granny insane. Maybe it did. She was always on her own, sitting in that saggy old armchair with the red blanket cover, staring at the log-burner.

Act 2

Everything's patterned in this place, old-fashioned, never matching – it would give me a headache if the lavender hadn't already. I open the living room curtain, let in some fresh air, and reach for the bunch hanging off the rail. It's tied up with brown string and decorated with dust and dead flies, nice.

By the time I'm done with the lavender, there's half a bagful and I collapse onto the sofa, where I always used to sit with one leg tucked under.

I started the performance weeks ago, playing Responsible Family Girl, and Mum handed me the key. Easy enough. It was just egging up my own boring personality – hardly an Oscar-winning performance. No, that will come later.

What shall I be in St Ives?

My name is Delilah, Queen of Allurement.

Or perhaps a wild partygoer, socialite, intriguing... something.

It's hard to come up with anything sensible with her empty chair looking across at me. Is there a hint of disapproval in the crinkled corners of the red blanket? No, of course not. The disapproval died with Granny.

I can see me now, ten years old, feet up on the sofa, telling her my idea.

'I'm going to be an actor,' I said. 'A famous actor.'

'Oh?' She didn't feel the need to lean forward, barely a crinkle of the forehead's acknowledgment. 'How do you plan to do that then?'

'By acting,' I said. Simple.

'Hmm, perhaps you could do the school show this year.'

'No.'

'Well, that's the sort of thing an actress does, isn't it?'

'The other kids hate me.'

She leant forward then. 'I'm quite sure that's not true.'

That annoyed me, that did. How could Granny be sure of anything? I only saw her a few times a year – five hours from London was hardly day trip distance.

'And besides,' she said. 'Why would you want to pretend to be someone you're not?'

'It's easier.'

Granny shook her head. 'Act if you must, dear, but it won't make you happy.'

Thus spoke the woman who died alone.

Act 3

I balance my orange makeup bag on the edge of the bath. The bathroom mirror is too small, and it's got a whole lot of smudges, like someone's been flicking their toothpaste. Never had Granny down as a toothpaste-flicker, but it suits me fine not to see myself clearly. Maybe I'll clean the mirror when I'm done working on this ugly mug, ready for the big reveal...

My name is Gwendolen, a Scintillator in Sparkling Jewels.

Well, I would be if I had any. Sticking with makeup for now. Makeup and a little denim skirt with a black T-shirt. Do I look like a child? Maybe I look like a child – an unpopular one at that, which is not the vibe I'm going for. I've played pathetic loner for long enough, since the day I was born probably, not that I can remember that part.

I'm off script again, keep focused, Glamorous Gwendolen.

I'm having doubts about Gwendolen, actually – she's gone and poked me in the eye with the mascara wand. Well, this eye will just have to be even more smoky then, won't it?

I laugh into the mirror, then hold dead still while I draw red around my Cupid's bow.

'Mum says I can wear makeup when I'm fifteen, but the other girls do already,' I told Granny once. 'It's not fair!'

'Of course it is.'

'No.'

'You're lovely how you are.'

38

My lipstick stops.

'They call me ugly.'

'Then why do you want them for friends? Choose people who love you for you, not for paint.'

Upper lip done, like a red moustache. I rub my lips together. Ugh, my stabbed eye is going all pink – that's not what I need for my crazy night out.

'You're not ugly, don't listen to them.'

Shh.

Act 4

I walk towards the front door. I might need a coat. Darn it, Granny, sort out the draught! Oh wait, you can't.

Back in her bedroom, I pick up my swishy black jacket, which was splayed over a chair. And something makes me stop: an embroidered box sitting on top of her chest of drawers.

A jewellery box. I really do need jewellery. Scintillating.

'Stop running around in circles and be yourself.'

My name is Devil. I look around me – like anyone's here to notice – and open the box's heavy lid. One plain silver necklace.

It sits on a pile of envelopes. I open the first one, marked with a foreign stamp, yellow and musty – deffo not urine. It's like I'm in a film, you know the loud crinkle sound when someone opens a letter, because it's near the mic or something. Loudest thing I've heard all day.

Dear L, I hope you are well, and all your family. It was wonderful to finally meet you in person.

Tanzania.

I moved on to others, all jumbled up, some old, some new. From all sorts of places, all sorts of people, all sorts of handwriting. Wow, Granny.

I put them back, quickly. The plain necklace is hanging over my palm. Hardly scintillating, but it's got to be better than nothing. Mirror? No, there isn't one in here.

'Beauty is only skin deep. You don't need to play their game.'

The bathroom mirror really gets my goat. Stupid toothpaste. Hair, what the heck you doing? And what is that face?

The girl looks sad. Sad and pathetic, painted up like a clown. She fumbles with the necklace's tiny stiff clasp, and finally gives up, dropping it next to the purple soap.

I sit down on the edge of the bath and…

CRASH!

The orange bag is upside down. Eyeshadow has exploded, like brown dandruff on the beige tub, foundation bottle rolling towards the plug hole.

I feel them coming, try not to blink, picking up a piece of loo roll and dabbing the corners of my eyes. Don't want to ruin my makeup. The stuff on my face I mean – my actual makeup is trashed.

I let the tears go in the end. There's no stopping them. I try out a crying sound, remembering I'm alone, and get louder and louder and louder. ARRGH!

Silence.

Then a whimper. Because that's what I am, a quiet whimperer. And I'm tired. Really tired.

I pick up the loo roll, slowly wrapping several sheets around my hand, and run the wad across my face. Tears are cheap makeup remover. Black, brown, and clownish red.

Darn you, Granny, you and your contentment, your stinky lavender contentment.

Act 5

The lit fire adds to the smell. Smoky lavender. No, no, I didn't burn them – that would be wrong, she wouldn't want it. I took them into the garden instead, black bin liner billowing as I shook them out.

Still, the smell lingers in here. The breeze is too chilly for me to keep the window open. I spray the mango again, but it makes no difference; lavender's been here longer. There's a bunch I missed on the hearth. Above, on the mantelpiece, are photos – of family, and of people in exotic places, the ones from the letters who chose to be part of her life, even millions of miles away.

Hello, everyone, I'm Lavender. I was named for my grandmother, a surprising woman who I miss every single day. If she were here tonight, she would tell me, 'Stop now, dear. Be still.'

I sit in the saggy old armchair with the red blanket cover, staring at the log-burner, with its lovely crackling wood. My bare legs are bumped with cold. I draw the blanket tighter. Maybe I'll sit here forever. I breathe slowly and deeply, letting the warm scent run through me.

Unspoken, Unheard

No, you may not switch the chips for spinach, or remove the sauce, or double the amount of chicken. I won't say this, of course, because the customer is always right, blah blah blah. And as we all know, speaking the truth doesn't result in big tips.

You're welcome, kind Sir. Merrrrry Christmas. And thanks, you're pretty too. In fact, that's all that really matters, isn't it? Even after I agree to constructing your sad little meal, you absolute—

My mum used to say if I didn't work hard at uni, I might end up cleaning toilets. Well, I'm working hard at uni, and cleaning toilets sounds divine. Lock the cubicle door, spray lemon stuff at the bowl, headphones on…

Focus, Trixie.

Wait, you're not ordering yet? Then why do I have to please wait a moment please dear?

No, the olive bread isn't gluten free. Bread contains wheat; wheat contains gluten. Does it say gluten free anywhere? Erm, nope, it doesn't, you—

I don't need to check with the kitchen. Admittedly, I've only worked in Wetherspoons for three hundred years, give or take holidays, so what do I know?

I'll check with the kitchen. It's the only way you'll let it go.

What now? Oh, the rest of your party will arrive soon, they're just finding a place to park and will be here as soon as possible. Good, that's delightful to know. I mean, the room is full of people with lack-of-festive cheer who are eying me up, ready to order, but I'm all ears for your late-arrival stories.

Of course, I shall get your double espresso decaf without delay. What the hell? Did I hear that right? Double espresso decaf... There's no tip big enough in the world to make that drink okay, you—

Great, just when I think I can escape, the door swings open hard. Those are some confident sons of—

The late-arrival party. Hello, hello, kisses on cheeks, this is our table, you go here, I'll go there, hang on dear we'll do our drinks order. Haven't I hung on long enough, Double Decaf?

Diet Coke... Sparkling Water with Lemon and No Ice... Just Water Please... And Another Water Please... Could I Please Have Half Lemonade and Half Orange Juice?

No, Sir, I don't need to note your Double Decaf. It's etched on my mind for all eternity.

No, this isn't my chosen career – thank you.

No, not Psychology... or Art... or Music. What a fun game! Keep guessing. It will never occur to your puny little minds that Law students need to eat too. Or maybe it's my 'prettiness' that's putting you off the scent. Either way, wasn't there something I was meant to be doing? Ah, yes, my job. And you can stop fidgeting, Diet Coke – I could have got you three drinks by now if Double Decaf and Just Water Please would stop trying to keep me here to look through my shirt!

Freedom, sweet freedom.

Thought too soon. Don't you click your fingers at me, madam. Why don't you try looking for the toilet before asking – it's literally in front of you. Do I look like a tour guide?

Yes, I can go back and get you some more ice, Just Water Please. My absolute pleasure.

Finally, a few minutes away from the Table of Doom. So happy right now.

All good things etc. Are you ready to order?

Do you need a little more time?

Of course you do.

I have a ground-breaking idea. Why don't you start studying the menu before the waitress is hanging over you with a notebook? No? Well, I thought the idea had potential. This is the table where time stands still. At least I'll have time to serve about ninety other people.

No, that's fine. Writing down, scribbling out, writing down. I could do this all night, and at this rate, I'll have to.

Umm, no, I've already put the order through.

You're welcome. The chef loves chucking perfectly good food because you forgot your dairy allergy. And he won't give you a roasting (pun fully intended) – he's got me for that.

It's not my fault, Julian. Fate has been cruel to all of us tonight. Stop yelling at me, you sweaty moron! Caught between a crabby chef and the Table of Doom. Oh, to be a cleaner...

My wrists are gonna break one of these days. I can feel them bending under the steak and chips.

Here's another idea. Just humour me. When I bring up a dish and say, 'Spaghetti Bolognaise?', how about only one of you speaks so I can figure out what on earth's going on? No? Oh, for the love of—

There you go. Enjoy. Alone at last. Peace, glorious peace.

Everything okay with your food?

Miracle.

It's like a competition to see who can leave the longest gap between mouthfuls. Talking and laughing as if you're in a soundproof room, with no one to overhear your comments on work colleagues and family members and the 'dubious quality of the establishment'; Wetherspoons really isn't used to that kind of vocabulary, is it? Knives and forks closed. Distressing amount of food waste.

Anything else I can get for you? Say no.

Wishful thinking.

Yes, decisions, decisions. They're both nice. Look, strawberry shortcake or lemon trifle? Order, please. This is not a hobby. I don't like the apron, I don't like tying my hair back, and I don't like being this circus performer. Please order, just pleaseeeee.

Uh huh. Cream not custard, ice cream not cream, custard not ice cream. Sure, I got all that.

Umm, no? Strangely enough, cream is the dairy-est thing I've ever come across.

I'll check with the kitchen.

There you go. Yes, we managed to find fake cream from a murdered coconut. Enjoy.

No coffee? Never have I been so grateful to see coats donned.

Yeah, well, you know what, the time to complain was when I asked you if everything was okay with your food. It's out of my hands now – I'm not a time traveller. No, no, no, please don't put your napkin in the half-full glass, it's—

Great. And thanks for swiping the table with your dainty hands, Diet Coke – now try getting all that crap out of the carpet! Why not tread it in while you're at it...

Twenty pence is not a tip. Who raised you? I'll give you a tip, you—

Oh, you wanted to leave more? What a shame you're out of change, every single one of you. I'll just have to pay my bills with good intentions.

That's it, leave.

Fine then, leave slowly. The people trying to come in love the cold and are happy to wait for your royal heinous-es.

Tripped on the doormat. Haha.

Well, that's something, isn't it.

Ha!

Those Nice Suits

It was the only time he had caught me looking. He smiled and said hello. I wasn't prepared.

Sometimes we both took the 07:51 from St Erth to London Paddington. I was always early. As pathetic as this sounds, waiting at the station with him was one of the highlights of my week. We would sit on the bench to the far right of the station, knowing, unlike some tourists and less-experienced locals, which end of the train we needed. He was always early too. A member of staff in an orange hi-vis jacket paraded the platform as it began to fill, seemingly getting a kick out of telling people the rough location of Coach J.

One of the first things I had noticed about him was that he didn't wear a watch. I know that sounds crazy but hear me out. It seems to be a 'thing' in high-flying circles, to wear the most ostentatious, expensive watch imaginable, regularly releasing it from a shirt sleeve and frowning at its ostentatious, expensive face. It annoys me, because said person has usually been staring at a screen up to that point, a screen that displays the time clearly. But no, it must be the watch – look at me, look at me, I'm running out of time, I'm important, I'm busy, busy and important, my time costs more than yours etc. Anyway, there was none of it with this guy at the station.

I dubbed him Grey Suit. Unless the weather required a black raincoat, the grey suit was all I saw him in. Grey suit with shiny black shoes. I can't say I've ever been attracted to smart business types – I know too many of them – but this guy wore it well, by which I mean he didn't seem to place importance on it. He leant back on the bench without consideration of the potential splinters or residue of rain drops and crossed his arms without fearing sleeve-creasing.

Grey Suit had a pretty face; dark, smooth skin, and a neatly trimmed black beard. Nice ears. I like nice ears. He wore bright, jewel-toned ties – red, green, or blue – a flash of life against his white shirt, always worn loosely at that stage of the morning. Not very tall. Neat figure. Arms that were not strangers to the gym but neither did they live there.

It was not his looks that grabbed me the most, before you accuse me of shallow objectification; it was his manner. Even with my sneaky glances and peripheral scanning, I could tell he was a nice person. He wasn't choosy with his eye contact. His eyes were eager to catch other people's and share positivity, chatting to anyone who was up for it, from cleaners to stuffy businessmen to lads with glazed eyes. He would have talked to me regularly, I'm sure, if I'd enabled him to break into my bubble.

I wore headphones. Sometimes I listened to music. Sometimes I listened to books on Audible. Sometimes I listened to music and read a paperback. Sometimes I simply wanted to soften the sounds of the station, using the earphones as a barrier in the same way people sometimes wear sunglasses, to shut out the whole world as well as the sun. Sometimes I wore sunglasses too.

Even though I always wanted to speak to Grey Suit, I feared it. I try not to discriminate, but… he was far too pretty. Talking to pretty is a struggle. I knew my words would have tumbled out in the wrong order and it would've ruined the joy of sitting next to him. My best friend, Lucy, says I'll become more confident as the years go by. She's four years older than me and takes on a grandmotherly role, emboldened by leaving me in the previous decade. Maybe when my thirties hit, I'll become an adult who can talk to guys. I doubt it though. I'm terminally pathetic.

A few years ago, Lucy and I were going on a shopping trip to the big city. Arriving at St Erth in the early morning without having eaten any breakfast, we popped into the tiny station café. The walls are covered with nostalgic Cornish memorabilia. There are three small tables and you can wreak havoc if you like to shove your chair back with no warning. It was full that day. We went up to the counter, cluttered snacks squeezed into baskets – chocolate bars, crisps, biscuits, fruit, cream crackers, all marked with handwritten labels on fluorescent cardboard stars.

'Two lattes and two bacon baps, please,' I said to the lad, through the serving hatch.

'Good choice,' he said, smiling. 'Can't beat a bacon bap.'

I smiled back. He had nice eyes, big and brown, and light red hair. Pretty. A little scruffy.

'Nice weather,' he said, tapping on the counter in the little kitchen, waiting for the chug of the coffee machine.

'Yeah.'

Lucy was quiet behind me. Unusually quiet.

'Where you headed?' he asked, handing us the takeout cups.

'London,' I said.

'Cool.'

He flipped the bacon on a little grill and chucked it onto the bread, spread with a thick layer of margarine.

'That guy liked you,' Lucy observed, when we stepped outside, holding the big baps together with flimsy napkins.

'No, he didn't.'

'He totally did. Couldn't stop smiling at you. Plus, we never get that many rashers normally.'

'Rashers? Sounds yucky when you say it like that.'

'Haha.'

We finished our food, chucked the napkins in a bin, and I brushed flour off my hands.

'Do you think I should talk to him then?' I asked.

'Yes. Do it. Buy a snack.'

I marched back in before I could talk myself out of it and leant on the counter with its bunting-patterned cloth. My heart thumped. His smile returned. 'Hello again, how can I help you?'

'I need… chocolate.'

Blur of colour. I grabbed a bar at random.

'My girlfriend loves Snickers,' he said. 'Can't say I'm keen. Peanuts. They make me queasy.'

So, that was that. I'd been rejected without saying anything. Queasy without even eating the Snicker bar.

When I told Lucy, face burning, she said, 'Never mind.'

Never mind? You see, it didn't matter to her; Café Guy was just an option, someone to shrug off while looking for the next one. It was practice. She praised me for trying and I thanked her for making me do it and said she was right, it was good practice, murmuring the words into the lid of my coffee so that she wouldn't detect the fib. That tiny incident crushed me.

The day that Grey Suit finally caught me looking, all I had to do was say hello back. That's how it works, isn't it? 'Hello' turns to 'nice weather' to 'where are you headed' to 'London' to 'me too' to 'my name's Anna' to 'my name's what-ever-it-is' – from stranger to potential within a few neat sentences, his interest locking onto yours until you're both at risk of missing the train. I didn't say hello back though; I didn't remove my headphones; and I didn't manage more than a mild smile. Terminally pathetic.

If I'd known I wouldn't see him again, perhaps it would have been different – perhaps I would have been different. I often picture him on another train, an earlier one, or a later one, due to a shift in his working patterns, a promotion that he deserves because he's so conscientious and there is no one better when it comes to people management. I'm happy for him.

49

The station has become lonely for me. It never was before. I look up more these days, often leaving my book in my bag, studying everyone as they trundle by with battered suitcases. There are plenty of people around, all bleary and automatic, but they don't catch my eye, none of them do. Grey Suit would have.

It's a Monday morning in May. Warm and breezy. Quiet platform. I put in my headphones and continue to listen to a self-help book. I wonder if I should stop with the whole winning friends and influencing people thing and instead choose something with a title like *How to Get a Grip and Stop Being Pathetic*. There's a book that's dying to be written. I close my eyes. I miss him.

A moment later, I feel a movement. A navy suit perches on the edge of my bench, trying not to be intrusive, staring at his phone. He switches from Messenger to email, over and over, even though nothing new comes through. Suddenly becoming conscious of me, he moves his hand so that the screen isn't visible. He taps his brown-shod feet and glances left and right, as though waiting to cross a busy road.

Navy Suit has a gentler appearance than Grey Suit – soft light brown hair and a face that doesn't look like it could be easily frustrated despite the relentless fidgeting. Calm face in a twitchy body. Active. Strong in other people's crises and anxious in his own. Reckon he's nice, sweet, kind. Understanding. He has eyes that would be nice to catch, if I could.

I can mull it over as much as I like, and find ways to justify my consistent inaction, but the truth is, I've simply grown used to making myself invisible. It's easier. It's comfortable. Imaginary romances have a certain amount of charm. I can't do it forever though. I can't spend my whole life glancing at lovely strangers without talking to them.

The train rumbles towards the station. I quickly remove my headphones.

'Hello,' I say, as we both stand, my heart kicking my ribs. He looks my way, pauses, and manages a mild smile. That's it. We climb onto the train and head into opposite carriages. I take an aisle seat, placing my khaki backpack on the window seat; that generally keeps people away until I'm forced to give it up when the train fills later in the journey. I draw my laptop from my bag to do some work ahead of an afternoon of meetings.

My thoughts drift to Navy Suit. A mild smile. I'd taken him by surprise, tried to start a conversation at a silly moment. If I see him again, I'll say hello immediately, right as he sits down, and invite him to shuffle closer – or at least have both buttocks on the bench! That would break the ice. Navy Suit will say hello back next time; I'm certain of that. He'll be more prepared. I might still mess the whole thing up, jabbering on and showing too much of my weirdness in one go, but what does that really matter? At least it would only be momentarily pathetic. I refuse to be terminal.

Kiss My Stretchmarks and Call Me Tiger

We wander to the end of the beach, away from the sunbathers, and sit down on my fraying striped beach blanket. The turquoise and lilac Cornish sea rolls up the sand, flattening and darkening it. This should be my focus: being on a date in this beautiful place.

Daniel's warm sweaty hand finds mine. 'Swim?'

'In a moment,' I say, stretching out my podgy legs. My long dark hair curtains around my face. The bright green kaftan reaches down to my knees, covering most of the problem.

'Okay.' His strong chest twitches. He releases my hand and brushes a fly away, before lying back, propped up by his elbows. Closing his eyes, he tilts his face towards the sun.

Now is the moment; I can do it unseen, slide my defence off, rearrange myself before he notices.

It's done. The silky kaftan pools beside me and touches his leg. Daniel notices instantly, half opening one eye and then both, squinting. I crush a handful of sand and count a silent tick, tick, tick… Will I reach four before he sees I'm disgusting? Five before he says it?

It had seemed such a simple thing: Yesterday told me something that it never should have, pressurised me when it had no right. *Wear the bikini*, it said. *He liked you enough to ask for a second date*. I'd turned to the mirror. *You are beautiful; you don't care what anyone thinks; you are beautiful as you are.* But Yesterday lied and Today is killing me.

Daniel twists onto his side to face me and reaches out, following the lines on my stomach with fingers that had only ever felt my hands before. I'm hurt by their gentle touch, physically hurt; it spreads up my stomach, shoots through my chest, and forces out through my throat: 'No!'

His hand jerks away immediately, because he's a good man. All the girls want a man like him – and once he's realised his mistake, one of them will have him.

'My sister has those,' he says. 'My mum, too.'

'What?'

'The…' He gestures to his own smooth stomach. 'The line things.'

'Oh.'

My skin had stretched, not during a pregnancy but during my explosion into teenage-hood, breaking into burn-like ridges on my tummy and arms. The marks would never fade. Disgusting.

He frowns. 'Sorry, I didn't mean to…'

'It's okay,' I say.

It's not okay. I'm not okay. But he's the okay-est person I've ever met.

'Swim? It'll feel much better once you're in,' he says, glancing back and forth between me and the water. 'You'll see.'

'In a moment.'

I sit up, slowly, feeling the stomach rolls form. He leans over and gently kisses the stretch marks on my upper arm. This time, the gentleness leaves no more than a hazy burning sensation, which quickly rises to my cheeks.

'You hot tiger, you,' he murmurs into me.

'Stop it, silly boy,' I say, trying not to laugh.

I don't want him to stop it though. Not ever.

He pulls away, smiles, and leaps up. 'Let's go!'

I drag myself up from the blanket, its edges flipping in the breeze; I pin it down with my bag. The turquoise and lilac sea smiles at me. It's not bothered by anything; neither is he.

There's a crinkly sunburnt woman along the beach, splayed out, letting the sun have its way. She opens her eyes when a group of young men pass, obliviously kicking up sand, some of which lands on her feet. She doesn't even bother reacting. No big deal.

Daniel's waiting for me at the edge of the frothy shallows. 'Come on, tiger!'

'Just a moment,' I say, adjusting my bikini bottoms.

This time, it's a short moment. A new feeling spreads through my whole body: the joy of being on a date in this beautiful place. I gather up my hair, tie it into a ponytail, and follow him into the sea.

When the Tour Guide Still Smiles

Paris. The city of love. Eiffel Towers everywhere, couples kissing for selfies, visitors buying fridge magnets from street sellers. It will help.

Tourists crowd the ramp to the Seine, waiting for the rope to be lifted. Four people beat us to the front even though we arrived first. They don't suffer from Britishness.

'I told you we should have got in the queue sooner,' she says, wrapping an orange scarf around her neck.

'Sorry.'

I worry for Becca in her thin blue dress, clinging just above her knees, and her feet squished in heeled sandals. It's not the warmest evening. I won't try to give her my jacket though – she finds it offensive.

'The Seine is like melted chocolate.' I touch her back, feeling the zip.

'Brown, Graham,' she says, shaking off my hand. 'It's brown.'

I'm a Paris virgin; nothing is 'brown' in Romance Central. People celebrating anniversaries, agreeing where to eat for the first time in years, falling in love, flirting, and not caring that lattes cost five euros. Five euros is barely anything these days, Becca.

The cool breeze brings an odd smell. Cheese? Garlic? Something someone shouldn't be smoking? I want to ask her. She'll know, she always knows. She's been here before.

Perhaps that's why she was so irritable last night – it could never be as exciting for her as for me. I was in a trance all the way up the Eiffel Tower, living every romantic movie I'd ever seen and wanting to create one of my own. I told her I would say 'I love you' on each of the six-hundred-and-sixty-nine steps. She said six is more than enough, thank you, so that was that. Sorry.

They unhook the rope and we surge onto the huge tour boat. How does Becca move so quickly in those heels? She doesn't look back. We climb the steps to the top level, fixed on the prize, all wanting a Titanic moment at the prow. I'm being overtaken and undertaken by Americans – or Canadians, perhaps, I'm never sure.

'Damn it,' says Becca, turning, her long auburn hair swishing.

The front rows are taken.

'Never mind,' I say, then close my mouth, not wanting to spoil the moment by panting for oxygen.

Her frown makes her eyebrows wonky, but that's how I like them best – sisters not twins, as she says. She raises them. 'Take your time.'

It's 8pm and the city lights are starting to twinkle, though it isn't dark yet. We take a seat in row four.

'*Bienvenue*. Welcome,' says the tour guide. She is like a marriage officiant, facing us from the end of the aisle; a young lady, about my age, in a well-fitted black suit, holding a microphone and wearing a smile that reaches every part of her face. 'I am your tour guide today and I hope you will enjoy what I have to say.'

She says everything in French and English, barely pausing in between. A plump woman across the aisle asks if she will use any Spanish – the tour guide tilts her dark-haired head and apologises. The Spanish lady doesn't understand the apology, in either language. The scenery speaks for itself though, as does the enthusiasm of the tour guide which increases every minute. How can anyone love their repetitive job so much?

'And now, coming up on the left, is one of the most iconic sights in all of Paris...'

'When the tour guide still smiles, there's hope for the world,' I murmur to Becca.

'Huh?'

'I said, when the tour gui—'

'Ooh, look!'

Notre-Dame. Everyone on the packed tour boat is startled, as if the towering cathedral is a monster about to swallow us whole. People stand to take pictures as we pass.

'I can't see the stupid thing.' Becca lifts her phone, trying to find a gap.

'Don't worry, there are plenty on Google,' I say, nudging her.

'Hey, don't jog.'

I sit quietly, waiting for her to finish, by which point *Notre-Dame* is behind us. Becca draws the orange scarf around her shoulders. She has goosebumps all over her arms and legs – her clothes are purely decorative.

'This is pretty silk,' I say, stroking the material above her knee. She changed from a denim skirt when we freshened up in the hotel.

'It isn't silk.' She twitches, always ticklish, and grabs my hand. 'It's made to feel like silk.'

'What is it then?'

She shrugs. 'Check the label.'

I don't check the label.

Becca tuts at a blurry photo on her phone, swipes to a sharper version of the cathedral, and gives it a dramatic filter. She's replying to messages now. Facebook is having a wonderful Paris weekend.

'Look, so beautiful,' I say. The sun is snuggling down beneath the city skyline. Ahead of us is a bridge, lit with warm lights. 'Magical.'

'Uh huh.'

'This bridge is called *Pont Marie*,' says the tour guide. She lowers her microphone, pacing slowly up and down, waiting for the right moment to speak. When she raises it, her eyes are bright, connecting with everyone who looks her way.

'This bridge is for the lovers,' she says. 'It is an ancient tradition that couples who travel beneath it for the first time must share a kiss, and their wishes will come true.'

'I've been under it before,' whispers Becca.

I touch the tour guide's arm. '*Excusez-moi*, is it the first time you go through with the person currently next to you, or the first time ever?'

She shrugs. 'I don't think there are any rules.'

'There aren't,' agrees Becca. 'It's not even a proper tradition. I read that on Wikipedia.'

'Well,' I say, kissing her lips. 'I believe it.'

'Of course you do.'

The tour guide looks my way for a moment. 'Don't forget to make a wish now.'

I wish everyone smiled as much as our tour guide.

A man stands at the front of the boat, leaning against the rail. He holds his phone in one hand, a beer can in the other; no ring on his wedding finger, no partner, no sadness. He seems peaceful. He doesn't appear to notice anything the tour guide says, but perhaps he can't understand, like the Spanish lady. Perhaps his eyes are happy to simply search the skyline.

Tour Eiffel. Applause breaks out across the boat when we see it rising from the city. I glance through Becca's phone, which can never truly capture the scene – it's like trying to photograph fireworks. The man takes a sip of beer, smiling. The tour guide is smiling too, always smiling, sharing the first-timers' joy.

'Yes!' Becca cries.

'What?' I ask.

'I've got a good pic,' she says, pushing the screen my way.

'Oh. Well done.'

I take her free hand, rubbing the back of it.

'You're sweaty,' she says.

'Sorry.'

I've apologised more this weekend than in the rest of my twenty-six years put together. As if I didn't feel British enough already, searching for proper toilets and trying to order a nice cup of tea. My deepest apologies. Perhaps I should phrase it like that next time; 'Sorry' must be boring her.

I wipe my palms on my jeans and cup both her hands, squeezing gently, before making use of my pockets. I'm starting to shiver now too. It's just as well the tour's nearly over. Becca is quiet.

The tour guide leans against the rail, microphone rested on her thigh, as we pull into the quay. There is a little jolt as the boat stops. 'Hopefully you have enjoyed what I've had to say.'

Most people are already standing up or fishing bags from under their seats.

'I have to tell you the truth.' She looks down. 'I am not a professional tour guide. I am a student, in Paris to work for the summer. Thank you for listening.'

Some of the tourists give her a clap. There's a funny taste in my mouth. Acid.

'Come on.' Becca gets up. 'We'll be here forever.'

People are already crowding the aisle, pushing their way down the boat with even more determination than when they got on. The way Becca's standing, the breeze is throwing hair across her face and she grabs it into a ponytail, long fringe escaping. She is staring down at me with the strangest expression, eyebrows more like strangers than sisters.

'Come on,' she repeats.

I stand, but there's nowhere to go yet. We must wait a little longer.

'What time we leaving tomorrow?' says Becca.

'Don't know.'

'Are we going from *Les Halles*?'

'Don't know.'

That's tomorrow's task. One of many.

When we finally get to the exit, we pass the tour guide who is standing with a donations box. I don't catch her eye. It's easy to smile when you're only here for the summer.

Becca draws her scarf tighter around her and turns. 'Are we walking or taking the Metro?'

Nothing can help.

She crosses her arms. 'Graham?'

My deepest apologies.

'Becca, we need to talk.'

Native

We must ask her where she's from. Kevin's certain it must be somewhere exotic. That skin, that hair, more Spanish than British, he says. We tut-tut. Everyone comes from everywhere these days, Kev – you can't possibly tell. We're all thinking it though.

The chapel is dark today. It's raining hard outside. Kevin suddenly remembers something and off he goes, scatty as ever. We wind lights around our tree at the front by the altar, decorate each windowsill, removing the cobwebs as we go, and try to find the tall candles from last year. It's always us who does these jobs. Our hands are busy, but our minds are free to wander – our thoughts rest on the new girl, whom we've only met once but she was keen to help. She bends over a box of decorations, hitching up her grey jeans and pulling down her red jumper to cover the gap, takes out some gold glittery baubles, and eyes up the table with the hymn books near the entrance. We don't decorate that. Someone should tell her.

We know her name: Seren. We had to lean in to catch the word. Welsh for star, apparently. Similar to 'seven' but an 'r' instead of a 'v', she told us that first Sunday morning.

Maybe she's just Welsh then, Deborah says. Welsh Celts can be dark, you know, just like us Cornish. Have I ever told you that my great-grandfather was Welsh? Yes, Deborah, you have. Many times. You're not Cornish though. Neither are we.

I'm going to ask her, says Carol, dropping the end of the tinsel that Deborah's wrapping around our tree. Carol walks up to Seren, who has finished placing clusters of baubles on the table (not a bad idea really) and is now balancing on a step ladder – that girl is a brisk completer-finisher. Kevin hands down the giant nativity figures to her, which are for our outdoor crib. We usually leave that job to the men, most of whom are unblocking drains and putting up the outdoor lights. Deborah claims that heavy lifting and standing in the rain aren't jobs for women because we're too delicate. Speak for yourself, we murmur. She's only Delicate Deborah when it suits her...

The nativity figures are rather heavy though. The Virgin Mary has a cracked nose from when she was dropped last year. They ought to be kept on the ground floor, we always say; it's ridiculous to have to lug them up and down. And yet they're always returned to the heavens in January.

We're done with decorating, so we all drift towards the ladder too, encircling Seren. The Virgin Mary is safely on the ground, thank goodness, and Joseph is being placed into careful arms. Seren squats to the floor to put down the figure. Carol judges this a good, safe moment to say: Good job, lass. Where you from?

Abrupt as ever.

Seren laughs, passing the back of her wrist across her face, smudging a fallen speck of mascara into her cheek. Hmm, good question, she says. Difficult answer.

Where were you born? we ask.

Wales, she says; I've lived there all my life.

We smile and say, Well, then, you're Welsh!

She frowns a little, wobbling on the ladder. Well, I'm only a quarter Welsh by blood – Mum's mother was from South Wales, Mum's from London, as is my dad, but Dad's father is from Devon and his mother from Cornwall.

We're sorry we asked.

Kevin hands Jesus to Seren. Done. They both seem relieved to return to the ground. Kettle on? says Carol, trotting off to the kitchen before we can reply. Deborah delegated the window displays to Carol but is now rearranging the holly in her absence, because it was wonky.

And now it's getting wonkier. There's no use saying anything.

The men return to the safety of the chapel, dripping wet. The Reverend Michael flicks soggy hair off his forehead. He's Cornish. As Cornish as pasties from St Ives. Right, he says; carols. Yes? says Carol, suddenly appearing in the kitchen doorway, leaning against the frame. She loves saying that. Every single year.

Rev shakes water off his hood and manages a smile, trooper that he is. Which carol do 'ee want? She can never think. The rest of us put in our bids; Silent Night, Good King Wenceslas, Hark the Herald, Deck the Halls with Boughs of Holly… Falalalalaaalalalala.

Rev nods and makes notes on a soggy-edged notebook, too big to be fully protected by his raincoat pocket. Right, he says, We be alright for they now. And finish as usual?

We nod. Seren looks puzzled.

We always sing *We Wish You a Merry Christmas* at the end, says Deborah, but in Cornish.

Oh! How does that go? she asks.

Re bo dhywgh Nadelik Lowen, says Rev.

It sounds like Welsh, she says. Only pronounced wrong.

Rev draws himself upright. Excuse me, the Cornish is the proper version. It's the Welsh that's pronounced wrong!

No, she says, crossing her arms.

Yes, says Rev.

No.

See, you are Welsh, Seren! Deborah announces. Completely Welsh. Just like my great-grandfather!

Seren smiles.

Tea or coffee? Carol asks her. She doesn't need to ask the rest of us – that woman is more gifted in the memory department than in Christmas creativity. She returns with a tray of mugs and mince pies.

We should practise *Re bo dhywgh Nadelik Lowen*, says Rev. Quick run-through, else it could be embarrassing in the service – not everyone do know it.

Mugs gripped between our hands to make up for the limited heaters, we begin. We still trip over the tricky words. Seren joins in, sounding as if she's singing a slightly different language, but we don't mind. It's Christmas.

Re bo dhywgh Nadelik Lowen
Re bo dhywgh Nadelik Lowen
Re bo dhywgh Nadelik Lowen
Ha bledhen nowydh da.

Seren is from Anglesey, Wales. Kevin is from Edinburgh, Scotland. Carol is from Yorkshire, England. Deborah is from goodness-knows-where, England – but her great-grandfather was Welsh don't you forget. The Reverend Michael is from St Ives, Cornwall. The baby Jesus lies on a blue chair, born in Bethlehem, displaced. We are from everywhere. And while the singing goes on, we are all natives.

Wayne's Name

The little girl in a silvery pink skirt had a skateboard hooked under one arm. It was almost as long as her body. Her knees and elbows were protected by black pads and she wore a pink helmet, clips hanging loose. She was followed by a woman with a pregnant belly that strained against a thin khaki vest. A man jogged down the pavement to catch up.

'Sorry I'm late,' he said, putting his hand on the woman's lower back. 'Didn't see your message.'

The little girl paused at the peeling red-painted gate that led into the skatepark. 'Mummy, why can't we go to the one near home?'

A group of teenage lads sat at the top of the quarter pipe, talking, laughing, pushing, and drinking. They scrunched their empty cans and threw them down the slope. One lad slid down with a whoosh.

'Go on, sweetie,' said the woman. 'I'll be right here.'

The little girl hitched up the tutu-style skirt and entered, holding the gate for her mother.

'So, how are you?' said the man. 'Have you got everything you need?'

'Yes.'

'Well, just as long as you're sure...'

'I am.'

'Good.'

They passed the gate and walked to the nearest bench, where they could overlook the skaters. The woman flinched as her bottom touched the green painted metal; it was a hot day.

She took his hand. 'Actually, I did want to ask you something.'

'I thought so.'

'Well, yeah.'

65

He ran his spare hand through his dark, grey-speckled hair, glancing at his watch as it passed his head, and drew his phone from his jean pocket. 'Just give me a sec.'

The little girl kept to the edge of the skatepark, looking left and right as though waiting to cross a busy road. Two boys skated while the others watched. They wore no protective gear. One was in shorts, knees covered with half-healed grazes. The little girl turned and put down her clean, un-scuffed board; its deck showed a picture of Spiderman shooting a web straight ahead. She sat on it, moving her hips from side to side, rolling the board back and forth, back and forth.

'Anyway, my question...' said the woman.

'So, go on then, what is it?' He sighed, stretching his arms above his head and interlocking his fingers behind his neck.

She jolted, hand flying to her stomach. 'He kicked!'

'That's good.'

'Here, do you want to feel?'

'I'm all right, thanks.'

'Huh.' She ran her hand over the bump. 'Doubt it.'

'Excuse me?'

The boy in the shorts cruised by on his back wheels. He grabbed the front of the board and landed on the balls of his feet. He looked at the little girl and smiled.

'Hey, you need some help?'

The little girl turned, and the boy glanced at her mother. 'Do you mind if I help her?'

'Sure, go ahead.'

The boy pushed wavy hair from his forehead. The skin was paler beneath. He crouched to her level with an arm wrapped around his board. It was bashed up and splintering, pale wood breaking through the black background and fiery print.

'Now, the first thing you need to know is this: you'll fall down a lot. If you wanna learn, you gotta deal with that. The main thing is that you get up and try again. Okay?'

'Okay.' The little girl fastened her helmet.

'Good. Now we can get started. My name's Darren.'

'I'm Lara.'

The boys at the top of the quarter pipe started to laugh. 'Pussy!'

Darren put down his board and rested his foot on it. 'Like this.'

She stood up and mirrored him, hesitating when both feet left the ground.

'Just try it and feel what's right,' he said.

She leant over, as if someone had kicked her in the stomach, and made the big step. The board shot from beneath her and she grabbed Darren's arms, landing safely on her white trainers. Lara let go and ran after her board. The seam of her skirt was edging towards the front; she twisted it back into place.

'Try again,' he said. 'Is it okay if I take her hand?'

'Yes,' said her mother.

The other skater whizzed by, holding his phone and performing a perfect 180.

'Don't look at him,' said Darren. 'Focus.'

The woman put down a backpack between her and the man. She shielded her forehead from the sun.

'Did you get my text the other day?' she said.

'Which one?'

'Ben...'

'Yeah.'

'Why didn't you reply?'

'Sorry.'

'I don't need you to be sorry; I need to know what you think.'

'Well, either's fine.'

'We're not talking restaurants.'

'You sure Lara's all right on her own?'

'Ben!'

Darren gripped both of Lara's hands as she tried again. His friends shouted obscenities and he told them to shut up.

'Bend your knees,' he said. 'Don't balance with your arms, balance with your hips. Like this.'

He rocked back and forth, as she had done sitting down. She nodded and tried again.

'Perfect,' he said. 'Now push off gently.'

Her legs juddered. She poked the ground with her toes, as if testing water temperature.

'Mum, look!' She rolled a few feet before falling, landing with a plasticky crunch on her knee pads. 'Mum, did you see?'

'I'm sorry, I didn't. Well done, sweetheart.'

'Well done,' the man echoed. 'Be careful.'

'I thought you might like him to be called Lawrence,' said the woman. 'You know, after your—'

'Hmm, I'm not sure what I think about Lawrence; it's not the sort of name for a baby somehow. That sounds silly I know, but what I mean is—'

'Fine. Fine.'

'Well, if you want to call him that, you can.'

'No, I've never really liked the name, but…'

'Okay, well don't name him on my account. I think something more normal, like Michael, would be better.'

'Michael?'

'Just an example.'

'Or Ben Junior?'

'You decide.'

Lara got on her board once again and skated halfway across the park, jumping off before she could fall.

Darren clapped. 'Nice one, kiddo. Don't think you need me anymore!'

'I do,' she said. 'Teach me how to go down the ramp, please.'

He followed her eyes. 'Hmm, not sure the quarter pipe is the way to go – you'll crack your skull open! Maybe try the fun box?'

He nodded towards a jump in the centre of the park, flat on top with shallow ramps either side.

'Okay,' said Lara. 'Show me.'

One of the other boys, who had a chaos of red hair, slid down the quarter pipe. 'Hey, Darren, we're leaving! You coming?'

'Where we going?'

'Shop.'

'Umm... okay.' Darren crouched to Lara. 'Sorry, I gotta go.'

'Thanks for helping,' she said.

'No problem.'

'Bye.'

'Be cool, take care.'

Darren waved to her mother. The lads walked away, leaving Lara alone. One kicked an empty can; Darren picked it up and chucked it in the bin next to the gate.

Lara trotted around the park, examining the halfpipe and the quarter pipe, before settling on the fun box. She lugged her board up the slope, leaning far forward and balancing herself by touching the ramp with a couple of fingers.

The woman looked straight ahead, fixed on her daughter. She ran her hands back from her temples, smoothing her already smooth hair; it was scraped into a tight shiny bun, either greasy or recently washed.

'I need to get back soon, Jade, or there'll be trouble.'

'Wayne.'

'Sorry?'

'Yes, Wayne. My brother's called Wayne and so's my uncle.'

'Really?'

'Well, I guess you wouldn't.'

'Wayne… Wayne… It's not a great name.'

Lara sat on her skateboard at the top of the ramp.

'Be careful,' called Ben.

'Hey, don't tell my daughter what to do.'

'Fine then, I won't.'

Lara pushed off, flying down and landing in a giggling heap at the bottom.

'See, she's perfectly okay.'

'Fine.'

'Will you please stop saying fine!'

'Okay.'

'Lara,' she called. 'Come here, please. Water.'

Lara wiped her forehead, tanned brown and speckled like an egg. She smiled, went up to her mother and slurped from a small pink bottle. Her neck bulged with each gulp. She wiped her mouth and exhaled as if it were the best drink she had ever tasted.

'Here, you're burning,' said Jade. She drew out a yellow-capped bottle from her bag, rubbed the white cream between her palms, and slathered it onto Lara's face and arms. She winced as it jolted her body.

'Mum, I'm going to do it.'

'Do what, sweetie?'

'Go down there, standing up.'

'Wow, you brave girl. Just make sure you don't break yourself – I don't feel like going to A&E today.'

'Look who's fussing now…' Ben muttered.

'Off you go, sweetie.'

Jade swiped sun cream over her made-up nose, leaving a white smeary mess around her silver nose stud; her foundation was a shade too dark and stopped sharply at her jawline. She and Ben watched in silence.

Lara's tongue slipped out between her lips as she prepared herself for the big attempt. Jade half stood when Lara hit the ground, and then sank down again, hand resting on her bump.

'I nearly did it!' said the pile on the floor. Her skirt had flipped up her tummy. She stood up, pushed it down, and tried again.

'Look, I need to know where we stand,' said Jade.

Ben put his phone back in his pocket. He leant forward and joined his fingers. 'I don't know.'

'You need to know. I need to know. I'm not a plaything; I'm a person.'

'You're a great person, Jade. You know that I… well, it's complicated.'

'Oh, please. Is that all you've got?'

'What do you want from me?'

'You know.'

'I can't. I'm sorry, I can't.'

Jade leant back into the bench, wincing when her daughter hit the ground again and took a little longer to recover.

'Jade, I… I have to go now.' Ben stood, slowly. 'I'll text you.'

'Sure you will.'

'I will.'

'And that's the way they do it these days, is it?'

'You're infuriating.'

'You're cruel.'

'Jade.' He took her by the wrist, and she retracted it quickly, leaving his hand suspended for a moment. 'Well, then.'

She glanced at him, then at the floor, then back at him. 'Ben.'

He turned. 'What now?'

'I love the name Wayne.'

He stood there for a moment, as if waiting for more. There was no more.

Ben walked away.

Jade pulled her vest down to close the gap. She leant as far forward as the bump would allow, pinched the bridge of her nose, and twirled her piercing. A tear made a pale streak down her bronzed cheek.

Lara stumbled up the ramp, looking as if she was losing control of her leg muscles after all the effort and falls. Wobbling violently, she stood on her board and pushed off. She reached the bottom of the ramp before falling, landing sideways and rolling.

'Mum, I did it!'

'Well done, sweetie!' Jade stood up, walked to the fence and supported herself with both hands.

Lara brushed the gravel from her body and looked past her mother. 'Where's Ben?'

'Oh,' said Jade. 'He had to go.'

'He didn't see.'

'No.'

'Aww.'

'It's okay. We don't need him.'

'Why?'

'Sorry, sweetie.'

Lara picked up her board. 'It doesn't matter.'

Jade watched the budding skateboarder give the fun box several more tries in the empty park, clapping every time. Lara didn't fall again.

Chanel No.5 on a Musty Woollen Coat

'You know when you walk into a posh hotel hallway, one with old red carpets, shiny stair banisters, and a smell of furniture polish?' you say. 'And perhaps the scent of an important woman who's just breezed through? It's like that.'

The Rosebud Tearooms must have sprayed the little silk bouquet on our table; it's old, a little dusty, but with a hint of perfume.

'I don't know.'

You won't let it go though. You feel the fake petals, gently rubbing them between finger and thumb, like someone trying to open a plastic bag without licking their fingers. It's as though the scent might be absorbed through touch and give you the answer.

I pick up the floral gold-rimmed teacup. My parents gave us this afternoon tea for our first wedding anniversary last year and the gift card expires today. It was good of you to make time, especially now your book is 'progressing well'.

'Well, it's not floral,' I say. 'Something fake and pretentious.'

'Hmm. It would be useful for one of my scenes, the one I mentioned earlier, where my protagonist feels displaced.'

A bestseller in the making, or a literary phenomenon, smashed out on a typewriter because you like the clickety-clack, and so do I; it helps me to know when I shouldn't talk to you, or bring a cuppa, or ask for help. I prefer to write my shopping lists on paper, with a 5b pencil. Soft and tactile. It reminds me of writing in the sand with a big stick at Porthmeor Beach, pressing carefully so it doesn't break – the I-heart-Tony of our brief honeymoon.

I bite into my jam-and-cream smothered scone – jam

first, the proper Cornish way. You haven't touched yours. I know you're still thinking about the scent, the best way to describe it. There's nothing else to talk about. I don't understand why with all the money in the world they couldn't have real flowers, replaced daily, and fill the room with Spring. Why the artifice, the slippery blooms drenched in privilege?

I catch the eye of the shrivelled woman at the next table and enter her head for a moment; she misunderstands our silence, thinking our relationship has soured.

'Chanel No.5 on a musty woollen coat,' I say, turning back to you. 'A coat from an antique shop or something.'

'What?'

'It smells like that.'

'Really?' You frown. 'Hmm.'

I wipe my mouth, leaving blood-red marks of lipstick and jam on the linen napkin. I fold it neatly and place it on the table.

One day, when I am a great success or win the lottery, I'll be able to afford Chanel No.5 and I'll spray it on a musty woollen coat from an antique shop. I'll force it under your nose: yes, the perfect description, but it won't matter. You'll never put it in writing. You'll never admit I was right.

'It'll come to me,' you say.

'Yes.' I rub my lips together. 'I expect it will.'

Half Dead but Whole Hilarious

The doctor says I'm in perfect health and have years and years ahead of me and I really don't need to make any more appointments unless I experience symptoms, but I know I'm going to die within the next few months, few weeks probably, days possibly, and those feelings are likely to be accurate given that my mother said with confidence she was going to die at forty-six, and died at forty-six she did, of a rare cancer somehow undetected, and I was forced to tell people 'told you so' on her behalf, because of course she wasn't around to say it herself, just like someone will have to say it on my behalf when I die within the next few months, few weeks probably, days possibly, from a rare insert-rare-illness-here somehow undetected, well clearly undetected because of the lack of perception from four young upstart doctors who wouldn't know the mystical truth if it slapped them across the face with a wet fish and will probably still insist there was nothing whatsoever wrong with me when I'm dead in the ground and that this is a total anomaly, a freak event, a freak event for a freaky woman, oh who would have thunk she would die at forty-six when there was nothing whatsoever wrong with her apart from her being. Dead. Makes sense, doesn't it, when all they can do is shove their heads into their big textbooks, the ones that are a font of all knowledge, and then, nope, slam them shut, nothing in there so it must not be a thing, sorry Mrs White, is there anything else we can help you with today, oh how about a nice little chat about burial or cremation, just to get ahead of the game considering you have no interest whatsoever in trying to delay the inevitable so might as well get all the bits and pieces in order like the funeral service, the reception the wake or whatever they call the afterparty, the fancy blue napkins for people to cry into that leave blue ink transfers on their sad ghostly faces as they say I can't believe it, I can't believe she's gone, she seemed so young and vibrant, only forty-six, gone just like that, boohoo, lively and fun and hilarious and now she's. Dead. What a shame she never had any children, no one to tell us 'I told you so', oh I'll rise from the grave in that case, rise rise rise like a fairy cake I will, oh told you so, told you so, told you.

When Seagulls

There was an upstairs flat on the road into St Ives with a seagull in its window. The man looked at it as he walked into town on Friday morning, a couple of hours after it happened. Paint was peeling from the window frame and underwear hung, like bunting, from a line. Someone hoovered inside, humming untunefully to a pop song on the radio. The carved stony seagull, with its wings clasped to its sides, watched the empty Porthminster Beach. The man looked away and quickened his pace down the hill.

I Gaz, you Deena. Aged seven then, both of us. Huge birds watching waiting. Your parents sprawl, five minutes flip five minutes flip, checking on their shiny fried chicken arms, five minutes flip five minutes flip, leaning on elbows with dogeared novels. You are yellow frock with blue shorts. Handstands cartwheels star jumps. Strawberry lemonade in plastic dome-covered cups propped by sand. Childhood tastes summer holiday salty beach. My parents sitting apart knees overcooked Yorkshire puddings far far apart glaring at the sea as if it had done something bad. I throw empty cup hard bounces on the sand turn for attention. A slapped hand. Put it in the bin up there do you hear me? Do you hear me? Yes Daddy. Do you want to destroy the planet? No Daddy. Then put it in the. Sorry. Recycling bin. Deena makes face takes slapped hand squeezes smiles drags me to the rocks away from dangerous plastic cups away from angry parents away from everything.

The man pushed open the heavy door of Marcel's. It was dark and tiny with a raised floor behind the counter, allowing them to see over the high shelves, packed with fresh fudge and Cornwall-stamped sweets. Susan asked what was wrong, arms crossed as tightly as a ribbon on one of the gift boxes. The man was silent. She asked him what time you call this and did you get lost or what. He remained silent. Susan asked if she was supposed to do everything around here or what. He removed his thin summer jacket and hung it from the hook behind the counter.

Nine then, both of us. Filling bottles with sand goal posts skittles hey Deena catch! Heavy. You dig sand grave for them. I say no take them all home stack them in our gardens big piles hills town mountains. We shouldn't fill the sea up. You shrug saying the sea's huge. I want to say it's getting smaller, discarded bottles bags choking strangling poisoning polluting death. Your blinking eyes caught by sun and sand don't understand. I say well okay then. Bury bottles for you, shame beneath the beach uncoverable by the next high tide. For you. Look out! Grab your hand. Ducking under swooping sea eagles.

We don't allow plastic bags in here, the man repeated. The young customer stared at him and asked if he was serious. He said yes, perfectly serious. She put it back into her pocket and tutted her way out of the shop, leaving a red box of Clotted Cream fudge on the counter. The door slugged closed. Susan appeared with latex-covered hands and said to please stop sending away customers, said at least the girl was reusing the bag, said we would make more money if people walked in and served themselves. No, no, they'll end up in landfill whatever. Honestly, Gaz, what you like? Please don't, he said, not today; they shouldn't be using plastic bags, will people never learn? She pinged off one glove and laid her hand on his shoulder. My sweet, sometimes we can fight these battles and other times we must accept that things are as they are.

Twelve then, both of us. Shape forming on your skinny body leaving me to catch up. Seagull's small glassy eyes stabbing sweet ice creams and vinegary chips. Careful

Deena says your dad, careful Deena says your mum. Your ice cream wrist loose bold daring. Until. Our parents sit silent serves-you-right looks. Your hand stays high eyes gripping the sky. It must be fun to be a gull you say, stealing food and swooping around. Entranced. Hand still raised empty. No they're sky rats nuisance to everyone and everything says my dad. You say you like them anyway. I tell you that liking or not liking is irrelevant sometimes and this is a sometimes. Sky rats. Taught you well says Dad. Mum slaps his splurging chest. Deena grabs my blue T-shirt saying you're a silly! Kiss on my cheek. Skips away down the beach. My body frozen but face hot.

Susan leant against the doorframe. A smell of warm butter and sugar drifted from the kitchen into the shop. She asked the man if he was going to tell her or what. He kneaded five-pound notes on the counter. Why they ever changed from paper is a mystery to me, he said; look how hard it is to iron out the creases! Tell me, she said; I wasn't born yesterday, you can't pull the wool over my eyes when you're rubbing money and muttering with a face that looks like someone died. Oh God, no one died, did they? The man opened the till and put the notes in with a final stroke – the twenties were starting to curl. And they're not biodegradable, he said. She frowned. Why would you want money to… degrade? He shut the till and looked up as another customer came in, an old woman with peeling burnt skin.

Sixteen or seventeen then, both of us. Upright in our deckchairs and shoes, too aware of consequences to put feet in the sand, too burdened for later's towels and soap. Hot day, big yellow circle showing her face. The sun is a woman I say, hurts you then leaves. The sun is a man you insist, hurts to look at it. The sun is female, pretty but causes damage. The sun is male, high in the sky and abandons you half the time. The sun is female, when she goes away she leaves you cold. The sun is male, everyone worships him but he leaves you burnt and miserable. The sun is female, big round and hot. Teehee. Pause. The sun is male, if you get too close he destroys you. Both bitter for no reason. I say men are very nice sometimes. Middle-aged frown on your acne-specked face, indoor hands timidly swishing through the white sand purple nails peeling. You look at me and out you blurt: We can't always be friends you know. I know what you want. I want it too. Always have.

Twenty-one then, both of us. Parents parading shops and cobbled streets. Us in deckchairs perched on the harbour, chips dipping ketchup. Birds pecking green bag Walkers' salt and vinegar crisps. Skywards surge. You say when seagulls fly they make you want to fly with them. I make you call them herring gulls Lord knows why like it matters. Love that, you say, herring gulls, I'll remember that, you're so passionate and knowledgeable, love that. Arms bridging from chair to chair fingers exploring fingers. Short hair phase bob tucked behind both ears. Prefer it long I say. She laughs throws a chip herring gulls swoop. Deena don't do that.

The man walked down the cobbled street to the harbour. A summer storm had flooded it a few weeks before, the new sea defence breached for the first time. Sandbags lay in front of shops and cafés. The man bought paper-wrapped chips. Sitting on a bench, he hunched forward, his free hand making a roof over his lunch – a circling gull decided against it. Once the man had finished, he stood up, scrunched the paper into a tight ball and chucked it into the mouth of a bin. He stared out to sea, hands gripping the rail. The tide was low, sun turning leftover puddles into mirrors. The phone rang in his back pocket. He whipped it out and looked at the screen. An unknown number. He waited a moment before answering.

Twenty-four then, both of us. Our own holiday new place new Cornish memory. Walking puffing panting along clifftop coastal path. Viewpoint overlooking Porth Kidney's empty stretching sands, bricks built into the rocks blended by crafty hands and the fierce sea winds. There and then before you can take in the ocean's purples and greens. Red flaky bare knee grinding into gritty concrete. You turn. Wait, what are you. Will you? Doing. Long blue sundress billowing, black bikini showing through. Birds squawking. Really? Yes, really. Marry me. An eternity it feels. Wipe of sticky forehead. You say yes. Yes!

The man wheezed up to St Ives Junior School; the hill was steep and the air heavy. When he found the office, the twins were waiting outside. They frowned and asked him why he was late and where had he been. Sorry, he said. So, you must be Mr Edwards, said the teacher – nice to finally meet you. We tried your wife but there was no answer. Is everything okay at home? The man took the twins' hands. Was there an emergency, Mr Edwards? I got Ava and Kai to school on time, he said. Anything you need to talk about? she asked. He shook his head. Can I help in any way? The man thanked the teacher for her concern and apologised again for being late and thanked her for her patience and said it wouldn't happen again. He pulled at his shirt, detaching it from his sweaty chest.

Twenty-six then, both of us. Patches in white-shirted armpits. Socks clinging to sticky toes. Dad's hand on my shoulder. Nothing but trouble these women, don't you forget they turn your head don't let her, look at me son. I look. Pale lifeless face of marriage bottled in a black suit. I love Deena I say. His sigh eats the room. Course you do. Hold to your values don't let her sway you. Yes Dad. Make sure there's a planet left for your kids. Yes Dad. Hold to your values. Yes Dad. Tie tied and retied straightened shaking hand mirror

81

smears and the weight of. I love Deena. Your joke the other night, a freedom funeral you called it. You tease you! Now focus, dum-dum-di-dum. Church waiting. I see you in white, first in my mind and then reality. Radiant. Hair long and flowing no veil. Smile faint painted in pink. Stretched walk dress scraping the ground.

When they arrived home, the man told Ava and Kai to please occupy themselves, please. He shut the door to their room and opened his own. He walked over to the big wardrobe, with its squeaky hinges, and fingered through the contents. There were more clothes than hangers; some were bunched up in twos and threes, the lower layers invisible. Bloody hoarder, he muttered. The man grabbed armfuls, heaving the hooks off the rail in one go, and dumped them on the floor, before turning towards the bed behind him, with its pink floral duvet cover. He sat down, reached under one of the pillows, drew out a pale blue nighty, and laid it across his lap. The twins burst in.

Twenty-eight then, both of us. Years of saving, deposit, mortgage, bring us back to happy place childhood memories fading dream. Houses below ours lapped towards uninhabitability. Autumn storms shrinking peninsula. Rallying. Save the planet save the planet save the planet! Check phone. Makeshift signs held high marching crusading down the street to wake up politicians bent in election lies and expenses scandals and patching holes in collapsing roads. No one listened to Noah and won't listen to us, stubborn animals snubbing the Ark. Check phone. Deena alone Royal Cornwall Hospital waiting for scan. Rain falling floods rising hold to your values hold to your values. Cold empty street November antipathy old lady scowling from Post Office at inconvenient protests. Check phone. Save the planet save the plane save the planet! Phone rings. Gaz you'll never believe it! What Deena? What is it?

The man looked up. The twins, still in their blue school sweaters, with hands on hips. They asked when they were going to have tea and what they were having for tea. He asked them to please let him be for a minute. Daddy, we've been waiting forever, said Ava. Forever, forever, said Kai. What are those badges? the man asked. Oh, said Ava, it says Protect the Environment. And mine says End Pollution Today, said Kai. The man threw the nighty off his lap. End pollution today and throw crappy badges in the recycling tomorrow, eh? Daddy, don't use bad words, said Ava. The man told her to stop being so bossy. Go play or something, he said; I'll be down soon.

Newborns then, both of them. Home delivery turned drama blue flashing lights thirty minutes ambulance squealing sick stomach stress. Gripped hand pain. And then. Shrivelled faces pink writhing one tagged with shoulder birthmark. Six pounds times two mother and babies doing well father off sick paternity leave blends into stress stress stress leave. Gaz hold Ava please I need. Environmental officer turns part-time sweet shop slave low paid benefits shame. To change Kai's nappy could you please just. Mother and babies all doing well. Hold her. Father and family all doing well well well save the planet hold to your values planet left for you kids. Gaz please!

The man lay awake the following morning, wrapped in his duvet like a sausage roll. There was a rumble of childish noise downstairs. He pressed his head into a flattened pillow, eyes squeezed closed, eyelids juddering. Gulls screeched in the chilly outdoors; the window was open a crack. He untangled himself, swung his legs out of bed, and looked out. The view was partially blocked by other houses, ones at risk of flooding, but a rectangle of blue sea remained in sight. The twins rushed in with plastic boxes on their heads, still in pyjamas at ten o'clock. Daddy!

Daddy! A herring gull has come into the house! The man rubbed his forehead. Please stop shouting. Please.

Two then, both of them. Screaming crawling crying. Deena covers her ears. Shh please shh. Screaming crawling crying. Deena get a grip will you. Twins tottering in opposite directions grab Ava's arm need both parents divide and conquer. I stand you sprawl on soft cushions collapsing under the weight of three previous owners recycle reuse repurpose. Deena! We need to go outside I'm suffocating Gaz please just please. Put on more clothes. No. And hats and then you. No. Can. They're kids they need sunshine like we did have you forgotten? We didn't understand and sunscreen is and the ozone and the earth and you do nothing and stop buying plastic! Cushion hits my face Deena croaks yells get away from the news the politics the scaremongers – I'm trying to survive the day Gaz why can't you see that? Selfish bitch what about our children's days the rest of their lives huh? You say life stopped long ago.

The man crept into the living room. A herring gull perched on the sill of the bay window, caught in a beam of sunlight. It knifed him with its eyes, as if waiting to see what he would do next. The man stepped back. I'll deal with it, he said, don't you worry, I'll deal with it. He stepped forward again. There was something hooked around the seagull's leg. A flash of red. Ava and Kai said not to scare it, said that it's probably gonna poop all over us. Oh, shut up, he told them, for the love of… shut up.

Five then, both of them. I grab the twins by their wrists drag them from the floor under the table raisins tipped out of snack bowls. Deena pinches her nose. Just let them play they can't be perfect all the time I can't be perfect all the time when are you going to realise? Don't be stupid. Don't say things like that Gaz that I'm not stupid you're a narcissistic psychopathic sadistic you haven't been taking your meds you. Stop buying these tiny plastic packets, get the dried fruit from. Great plan that shop's across town and you don't want me to use the car what am I supposed to do? Walk. With two five-year-olds in tow? Gaz I'm serious it's strangling me can't breathe we can't stop this thing on our. Grab your shoulders shake. Own. Not one bit of plastic will end up in the sea on my watch nor in the recycling to be dumped in other countries shifting the blame do you hear me? Ava and Kai will learn that this is not a game. Blood from your bitten lip. Seeping eyes.

The man turned to the twins. They sat on the living room floor, making towers out of a pile of clear plastic rubbish. Tomato boxes, blueberry tubs, toy containers... Ava stood up and withdrew her arm from a hole in one of them, the jagged edges making a powdery white scuff in her skin which quickly turned pink. Daddy, are you okay? She took his hand. He glanced back at the seagull. When is Mummy coming back? You said she would be back soon, and it's been forever. He told her that Mummy's fine and she'll be back, of course she will, don't worry. Kai, cross-legged on the floor, was dressing up like a plastic robot. Can you close the window, Daddy – it's too cold. The bright blue curtains billowed either side. The man said the fresh air is good for them and besides, the bird hadn't budged. Can we have the heating on? No, it's the middle of summer, it's a waste – put more layers on or man up or something.

Seven now, both of them. Film drama door slam. Bang! Gone. Long day long night no news children asking for you playing on the mountain of damage you've done. Gull glaring, taunting. You'd know what to do. You'll tell me where you are soon, tell me you're safe won't you. You'll come back for them soon won't you. Soon. Door shut on me our children the mission we could have shared if you'd had the strength. All in vain perhaps. But what is life if we give up, give in? You never wanted to know, never tried to be better than you were. And now. When seagulls fly they make you want to…

The man approached the window, slowly, tiptoeing. The herring gull pattered in circles, seemingly unafraid. The man leant forward and tried to touch its feathers; it shuffled away, foot caught by a red plastic ring from the lid of a bottle. Ava crept up. He grabbed the bird by the neck. It cried and wriggled, beak twisting towards his fingers. Ava started to whimper. He pulled the red ring off and then tightened his grip, harder and harder. Don't strangle it, Daddy. There was a whirring sound outside. I'm not, said the man. He peered out of the window. The whirr intensified. Daddy, stop. There was a flash of red and white as the RNLI helicopter flew over the house and towards the coast. Daddy! Don't yell at me, Ava!

The man flung the herring gull out the window. It hit the floor, stunned for a moment, before testing its legs and wobbly wings. Kai rushed up to Ava, clutching at her. They leaned forward across the sill, watching the bird try to find its balance in the wind. Daddy, you shouldn't have done that, said Ava, starting to cry; look, it's hurt. It's fine, he said, the bloody sky rat is fine. Within a few seconds, the herring gull had begun to fly, unsteadily, close to the ground. The man slammed the window.

The Ones I Never Sent

Subject: A Favour

Hello Caroline,

It was good to start working with you. I hope you settle in quickly. Could you send the copy over by tomorrow morning? Don't worry if you can't, but it would be great if possible. Thank you.

Best,

Mark

[Draft] Subject: Re: A Favour

Dear Mr Waugh,

Thank you for

Thank you from the bottom of my heart for working me much harder than anyone in their right mind wants to work, especially in their first week, when I wanted to sit with my head plonked on the desk swimming in hair and despair. You charmer you.

I don't suppose you could let people leave work at work, could you? No? Fair enough, we do get paid more when we take work home. HAHAHA! Good one. See, I'm funny too – pay rise? You know you wanna. It'll pay for these chocolate truffles, retrospectively, and next time I'll upgrade to Lindt Lindors. Thank you kindly.

To summarise this 'committee meeting': No, I will NOT do it before tomorrow. You can take work and shove it where

Yours insincerely and tipsily unbalanced,

Caroline

Arrgh, nearly sent that.

New message.

Subject: Re: Tomorrow

Caroline

Great, thank you. You're a star.

Best,

Mark

Subject: Celebration?

Hello Caroline,

I hope you're having a nice relaxing weekend.

I was wondering about having an office Christmas party this year; it might be a nice way for everyone to bond and have fun. Beth mentioned you've had some experience organising. What do you think? No worries if you don't have the time or inclination. Beth is happy to organise it.

Best,

Mark

[Draft] Subject: Re: Celebration?

Dearest Sir Waugh,

Yes, of course I'd love to organise a party for people I've known for five seconds. They can put me on trial for my life and it'll save me the trouble of getting to know them. You call these canapes, Miss Caroline?!

Thanks for recommending me for the job, Beth, but you didn't say I'd have to pay for it this way. Couldn't I have given you a foot massage or something? Eww, if that were the deal, I'd have to fire myself from the Best Friend position.

Experience organising?! One 30th birthday for an ex and you call that organising? Disorganising more like. He was a complete

Do it yourself if you're so keen!!!

From, Caroline

Subject: Re: Celebration?

Morning Caroline,

Thanks for your quick reply.

Are you sure? I know you're busy…

Best,

Mark

Subject: Partayyyy!

Heyyy Caz,

OK, so, Mark says you're planning the Christmas party woooooo! Lol. I'm here if you need help.

Though we could do decorations? I was looking at YouTube, creative stuff, with paper. What you reckon?

Beth xx

[Draft] Subject: Re: Partayyyy!

Dearest Bethany,

If you call me Caz one more time in the office, I'll knock your block off. I've told you a gazillion times to use my proper name at work. C.A.R.O.L.I.N.E. Why is that so hard, Bethany?! I know your name's Elizabeth, but I'll call you Bethany because I have NO RESPECT FOR THE SANCTITY OF YOUR NAME!

And please proofread your emails – it's 'thought' not 'though'.

Right, any port in a storm, as they say. And in the storm of no wine remaining, any port it is: Cockburn's finest.

Lots of love and disrespect,

Your bestie,

C.A.R.O.L.I.N.E

Oh, and stop twizzling your red locks every time the boss walks over. It's indecent.

Sincerely,

Everyone

Subject: Re: Partayyyy!

Heyyy Caz,

Awesome! Nahhh, tinsel's old-school – I'll see

what I can dredge up instead. Mark's favourite colour is red so I thought it would be cool if we had that as the them. What to you reckon?

Beth xx

P.S. Thoughts on drinks?

[Draft] Subject: Re: Partayyyy!

Heyyy Elizabeth,

It's Caroline, CAROLINE!

Oh, fine then, no tinsel. You win.

Way to go, 'bestie', way to kiss beep. Oooh, red is Mark's favourite colour, oooh. And what does 'if we had that as the them' mean? Oh, you meant 'theme', but obviously the spell check wouldn't pick that up. How do you even do your job?! I'm nose deep in Baileys and I can write properly.

What 'to I reckon'? I reckon… how do you know his favourite colour? Are we still in primary school or did I miss something? What's his favourite animal? Favourite shape? (Your face, maybe.)

Hmm… Red is nice, but you know what else is nice? ANY OTHER COLOUR. I like green, you like blue, that cow from downstairs seems to like yellow. Mark Mark Mark.

Kiss. Beep.

All my love and Irish Cream xxxxx

Subject: Re: Partayyyy!

Hey Caz,

Hmm, I dunno. Doesn't the red/green seem a bit clichéd for Christmas? I was thinking like red and gold or something. Anyway, I'm sure you know best, you usually do.

So, what do you think of Mark? I wasn't sure at first, but he kinda grows on you. Bit reserved. That makes him all the more fun to tease though, he sorta blushes in his eyes, you know what I mean? Bless him, he's good as gold. I'm trying to persuade him to grow out his hair a little, more short back and sides rather than short short short.

Beth xx

P.S. Let's go with tinsel actually... quicker and easier.

[Draft] Subject: Re: Partayyyy!

Hey Beth,

Oh yeah, because red and gold is the height of Christmas originality. Next you'll be telling me that gold is Mark's second favourite colour – it's not even a colour, it's a texture, just saying.

Leave the beeping man alone! It's up to him what he does with his hair, not you. Feminism works both ways, hun. It would look better a little longer though, can't deny it. Looks like an egg head. He's probably balding too. He doesn't need to make any changes to be Mr Popular though, does he? I hate those kinds of people. No effort. Like you, Beth.

Caroline xx

P.S. I SAID TINSEL IN THE FIRST PLACE.

Subject: Re: Partayyyy!

Yeah, he is, very bright and pro.

Beth xx

[Draft] Subject: whatever

Dear Beth,

'Oh Mark, it's so good to have someone who eats healthily in the office.'

What. The. Beep. Was. That?

Get your pretty face out of Mark's desk and stick it in your Tupperware tub of cous cous.

Love you, hun.

Caroline xx

P.S. He's not even vegan. I saw him eat egg sandwiches, hah!

Subject: Christmas

Hello Caroline,

How are things progressing for the party? Beth has

filled me in a bit. I'm sorry our conversation was cut short yesterday. In answer to your question, no, I haven't read The Unconsoled – I'll put it on my list.

Best,

Mark

[Draft] Subject: Re: Christmas

Lord Waugh,

How is it progressing, you ask? Progressing, progress, Pilgrim's Progress.

From, The Unconsoled.

Subject: Re: Christmas

Hello Caroline,

Wonderful. Don't work too hard. Delegate.

Yes, I remember hearing that Ishiguro was more experimental after The Remains of the Day.

Best,

Mark

[Draft] Subject: Re: Christmas

Your majesty King Waugh,

I'd just like to thank you for being so professional around me. It's a wonderful trait in a boss.

Regards,

Your loyal servant.

I should probably get a journal, instead of ranting my Draft Folder into a nervous breakdown.

From, Champagne-powered Caroline. (Don't judge, found it in the back of my cupboard.) xx

---

[Draft] Subject: hfgfbg

Arrrgh, Beth, could you PLEASE get your head out of your own behind, or Mark's behind. You haven't giggled that much since secondary school and even then, you looked and sounded like a nincompoop. I MEAN IT.

Send

Subject: Re: hfgfbg

Caz, Errrm what the? I wasn't giggling I was laughing because Mark said something funny for a change and if you weren't so uptight all the time you'd have been laughing too. I don't know why I even bothered getting you the job when you speak to me like this!!!

[Draft] Subject: Re: hfgfbg

Oops...

GETTING ME THE JOB? If I hadn't worked my butt off there's no way I would have been offered it so don't give yourself all the credit!

Subject: Beth

Hello Caroline,

I have had a complaint from Beth. She didn't tell me any specifics but seemed hurt by some things you said to her. I hope it was simply a misunderstanding and that you'll be able to rectify the situation with an apology. I wouldn't normally intervene, but we have such a happy atmosphere here and I wouldn't like that to be spoiled.

Best,

Mark

[Draft] Subject: Re: Beth

Are you kidding me, Mark?

Subject: Re: Beth

Hello Caroline,

I'm glad to hear it. Keep trying and I'm sure she will come around.

Best,

Mark

[Draft] Subject: Reply!

Beth, you SNITCH. Why would you do that? Avoid me all day and then go crying to Mark, that's the most infantile thing. And it's all very well marching off to the coffee machine when I try to apologise...

*bet you wish the machine had been working. HA!
Looked like a right idiot marching straight back
again. Two words, Beth: Flask. Bring flask.*

Well, you're not getting an apology now. I tried, okay?

*Please don't hate me, please don't. I need
youuuuu!*

*But if you FLIPPING WELL think I'm going to say
sorry any more, then you've got another thing coming*

cAROLINE

Subject: Re: Reply!

Hey Caz,

*Aww, no worries, apology accepted. I get it, Mark
IS a little intense. Would drive anyone to use there
bestie as a punch bag. Sorry if I overacted, love
youuu! I wanna go out tonight you coming? But
maybe you need to ease up on the drink hun? Lol*

Beth xx

[Draft] Subject: Re: Reply!

*Gee, thanks. ('There bestie' needs to learn how to
spell.)*

[Draft] Subject: sksjsjsksjjsffffffffffs

Dear Mark,

*Okay, that made me feel like a child. Not even a
detention; an expulsion. Take the afternoon off,*

Caroline, you need it. Well, whose beeping fault is that then?

It's normal to burst into tears at work and hit your head on the desk. It is to me anyway, but you're straight from problem to solution, wearing an annoyingly calm expression. Couldn't you be riled just once?

Subject: Hello

Hello Caroline,

I hope you're feeling better. It's a stressful time of year. Let me know if you need to take any more time off.

Best,

Mark

[Draft] Subject: Re: Hello

No, Mark, I'm not. I have a million things to do and no time and a boss breathing down my neck in a sympathetic but persistent way and a best friend who's doing my head in and an abusive relationship with coffee.

I forgot to mention the Christmas party! That's also a pain in the

Do you know what Beth said to me? I quote: 'Nah, Caz, I've changed my mind about the decorations. Tinsel is just too tacky.'

Ojosjosjofjsofjsofj!

One, tinsel is a cheap gift from heaven. Two, I've already bought loads in a shade called Mark's Favourite Colour. Three, who put her in charge of decorations?

From a disgruntled employee.

DISGRUNTLED. (Best word in the English language, apart from 'hibiscus'... but that's beside the point.)

Subject: Re: Hello

Hello Caroline,

I'm glad to hear it. See you tomorrow. Perhaps we could chat about party arrangements after work? Beth said she has a few more ideas to throw around, but I don't want it to all get too much for you. I believe she's compiling the playlist though.

Best,

Mark

[Draft] Subject: Re: Hello

I beg your actual pardon? Beth 'compiling the playlist'?!?! I've already compiled one with suggestions from everyone and she knows that.

[Draft] Subject: Party

Beth, put your hands above your head and STEP AWAY FROM MY DECORATIONS AND PLAYLIST OR I SHALL SMITE YOU.

Subject: Re: Party

Heyyy Caz,

No worries, my pleasure! Thought we could do with some songs that weren't so... ya know... meh. Who did you get for Secret Santa? I got that weirdo from across the hall, ugh.

Beth xxxxx

[Draft] Subject: Re: Party

My name's CAROLINE.

Secret Santa: clue's in the name, hun. Anyway, you won't be happy if you find out.

I really do love you, you annoying piece of

CAROLINE xx

Subject: Re: Party

Oooooh, what you gonna get him?!

Beth xxxxx

[Draft] Subject: Re: Party

Lord knows! Actually, I expect you know too, don't you?

You know everything.

Because you

KISS. BEEP.

XX

Subject: Re: Party

Suit yourself, I'm sure he'll love it. Nah, I did at first, but he gets kinda boring. He's just Boss Mark. Yawwwwn.

Speaking of... something different, I have my eye on someone at the mo. You know Kirsty? My cousin's best friend, you might have met her at the wedding that time? Green pencil dress, puffy legs, wrong shade of pink lipstick? Anyway, Kirsty has a hot brother. Called Gary, good height, strong, not a bad face!

Beth xxxxx

[Draft] Subject: Re: Party

Now you tell me...

What. A. BEEP.

So pretty and extroverted and interesting. I'd love to be more like you, except

Mark is NOT boring.

Caroline xx

―――――――――

Subject: Thank You

Dear Caroline,

Thank you for all your effort. Everyone said it was the best Christmas party they have ever attended. Well done. You deserve a Nobel Prize for canapé-sourcing. I'm sorry I didn't manage to talk to you much.

Thank you for the present, too. At least, I assume it was you. The Unconsoled doesn't strike me as the sort of generic item that anyone might have chosen.

Are you all right? You seemed even quieter than usual last night. I hope your head recovers soon; it must have taken quite a beating.

Best,

Mark

[Draft] Subject: Re: Thank You

Deer Mark,

The truth is you're so, friggin, beautiful. Your're awkward shuffling on the dance floor, the little smile creeping onto your lips, the glancing at the feet of your partners (who don't know how lucky they are) in case you clip their Gucci's or whatever, the gentle hand on their backs as you lead them off at the end of the song, so kindly, so respectfully, missing out none of the ladies, except me, of course, because I can't look at yoi.

ARRRGH! I'm not shy, I don't hate you, I'm not aloof, I like you!!! You're so NORMAL.

Caz xxxxxxxxxxxxx

Send

Subject: Re: Thank You

Hi Caroline,

Was this meant for me or for a different Mark? I hope you were still drunk when you wrote it because it contains a shocking number of commas, capital letters and exclamation marks. Don't get me started on the spelling errors. Didn't the serrated red lines beneath give you a clue?

Best,

Mark

Subject: Re: Thank You

Oh my gosh, that wasn't meant to be sent! I can explain I promise!!! Please don't tell anyone. It was a mistake, so sorry!!!

Subject: Re: Thank You

Hi Caroline,

No problem. See you Monday.

Best,

Mark

P.S. We could meet to discuss your intriguing ideas. Saturday, 10.30, Costa? x

P.P.S. Still too many exclamation marks, Caz.

Burning Me, Maybe

On Saturday October 1st, a young woman swam from Porthminster Beach and never returned.

You found out from her cousin down Norway Store; he said it happened early that morning. The pint of semi-skimmed soured. The KitKats started to melt in your hand. You searched for the right thing to say and came up blank. Pain emitted from the lad, and you caught it; it seared your palm through the crinkled receipt.

Your wife thinks you take things too hard, even when it's not your grief to carry, but the images were too strong to ignore. A joyful young woman in a black one-piece; a smile as she skipped down the beach for the last time; seventeen years dragged out to sea, just like that.

On Saturday October 1st, *a young woman like my precious Grace walked down to the sea, might have tested the water with her toes, declared it freezing, said it would be okay once she got in, as if that made it any warmer. If Grace had been her friend, she would have said no thanks, mate, not on your life, I'll hold your phone and towel. She would have seen her floundering, called for help, and then... but Grace wasn't her friend, and Grace is only seven, and Grace wasn't there. No one was there.*

And on... and on...

You decide you must murder your journal; each page, one by one, dipping the corners into the flames, holding them until the heat becomes too great for your shrivelled fingertips.

Saturday October 1st, a young woman swam from Porthminster Beach and never returned.

See, that's what happened, and that's what you should have written, but then you thought about it.

Ursula. That's all her cousin said. You made up the rest because, yes, you always take things too hard. Maybe she looked like Grace and maybe she didn't, and maybe she behaved like her and maybe she didn't, and maybe it doesn't matter either way. You could find out if you weren't too scared to give her a face.

On the evening of Saturday October 1st, you and Grace curl into a big armchair to read a story set far far away from the sea. She wriggles in your lap, grasping a red wrapper, her mouth smeared with KitKat chocolate. She nudges you to turn the page. Only a careless headline or newsflash could break her innocence; she doesn't know, and you'll never tell her.

Get away, feelings! They're as futile as the blank journal on your bedside table, the one you wouldn't taint with your words, because that devastating day had nothing whatsoever to do with you.

And yet… fire can't extinguish water, can it? Not waves, nor tugging tides, nor salty tears from grieving strangers.

No, try as you might, the feelings are still there, caught up in an imaginary fireplace. Those stubborn ashes say you matter.

She Went There for the Weekend

And I've reached your doormat. Standing on the bristly Home. Why am I? Should I? How will you? You won't have a clue why I'm. But you said anytime, sis, like when your hubby's fishing, you know where I am, gimme a call, pop by, whatever.

I didn't call.

You might be working late.

Well, I'm here now Cara but. Why am? Shh. Wait calm breathe. Oh just. Knock knock knock three is poetic, pivoting on the central point. Not that that's. Doormat. Feet wiping old mud new mud. Peeling sole peeling soul. Doormat. Shh. Please be home please be home please be. Don't beg three times like a needy little. Home.

Your wet weedy red hair flicking from the window. Jane I'll be a sec! Not too long a sec please is sticking in my throat. Just showering hang on! Hang on hang on, hanging like his fishing line from the riverbank. Sitting waiting endless patience for them. And then. Fish bite, hanging from the hook. He'll smile them from the water. Good catch he'll say. Do you mean the fish or? I fish compliments; he doesn't bite. Chucks the corpses on the marble for me to clean and slice. Wordlessly. Then off he goes to shower down and check his emails.

He'd got ready dour as death. Yes dear no dear three bags full dear. Yanking waders on grunting at the ankles. His keys his wallet his fishing stuff stuff it. See you later. No I'm going to visit my sister won't be back 'til late Sunday. Oh great idea you haven't seen her in ages have fun should have been his response. And then I wouldn't feel so.

Weekends wash it all away. That's why I'm. Family is family. Familiar broken black bag strapped across my body like a medal for all I've ever. Bought for me back when was it? Our eighth or ninth or maybe. Pocket zip scratches reaching in. Tissues. White fluff, disintegration. Tissued fingers grip my nose, tilting head to let it flow. Doormat. Poking it with chilly toes. Held together by my coat.

Door flung wide. You appear all damp and fresh. Plumper younger thirty-nine. I have twenty years on you, little afterthought. Twenty years of settling down becoming needed. Beaming smile eyes wide surprised. You let me in with no flung questions. Guiding me through trails of trash, uncared-for plants, expensive clothes strewn with labels still attached. Kitchen's worse, stinky cups from goodness knows, wine in lines behind the mess.

Can I make you a cuppa? You can; you may. Dear Jane just the same so what brings you? Milk no sugar please. You didn't answer my. Goodness Cara you've got to sort this mess. Yes yes but. Do you mind me visiting? No course not is this strong enough or. Lovely. Do your own milk. Plastic bottle red on top.

Armed with tea, weapons of mass. Biscuit? Please. Clearing a place to sit on the sofa; magazines, magazines. You should of told me you were coming then I could of. It's should have could have. Got some food in made a meal been a good hostess; you caught me off. I'm sorry. Guard. You don't mind though do you? Quit asking, I told you before, gimme a call pop by whatever. What are we going to eat then? Rotting lettuce dubious milk and some other crap that I'm scared to look at or we could go out for a nice meal.

He and I never go out for a nice meal. Always me who cooks. Not today. Today he is abandoned. He doesn't have his. Doormat. Wife to take care of everything. Scratches his head and cleans and slices. Olive or vegetable or butter? Low heat or medium heat or high heat? I can feel the burnt skin and raw middle and his saddened face. How could I go away and. Doormat. Leave him to fend for.

Let's eat out you say. What time shall we go? I ask. Dunno I'll think once I've dried my. Beautiful autumnal crown. Hair and see where there's a table. Fine must work to your schedule lack of schedule relaxed unfocused I can do this I can I can

1. take a deep breath in through the nose
2. out through the mouth
3. in through the nose, rinse repeat, until

I submit myself to the weekend.

Your favourite restaurant found us a table even though you didn't call them, just like I didn't call you. It's next to the toilet. Another diner nearly walks into me on their way past; too dark and cramped but will have to suffice.

How's hubby? you ask.

Okay, I think.

You think?

What dish would you recommend?

It's all good. I'm leaning towards spicy chicken.

I'm sure, I say. Is it too spicy or not spicy enough?

I don't know. So, what's he up to this weekend then while you flit off irresponsibly?

Fishing.

Lordy, he's a dull old git!

Please don't talk about my husband like…

Oh, but come on seriously.

…that.

The waiter saves us. Evening ladies, can I get you any drinks?

House red please, you say without a pause.

Please may I just have tap water? I say.

Sure, ice?

No, thanks.

You shake your head at me. Disgust for my black top and khaki trousers, perhaps. I didn't know we'd be going out. I don't have your red dress, falling above the knee, with its deep V-neck that narrowly stands the right side of appropriate. I don't have the hips to fill it out, or the shiny blue handbag, or the little mirror you take from it.

The waiter presents our drinks with a young-man flourish. Clean apron, good posture, a smile to charm our loose change.

You rotate the glass between your finger and thumb, trembling the deep liquid. Ever fancy a drink? you ask.

No, never – he doesn't, so I don't either.

That's silly.

I want to be supportive of his decision and I can't be supportive if I'm guzzling bottles of the stuff.

Lordy, sis. No wonder you're so thin and miserable – you never have anything nice!

Starchy silence. You finally put the mirror back in your handbag and peruse the menu because you never order the same thing twice. Salmon. It's fish-night back at home, so I almost go the same way, but my stomach says otherwise. Spicy chicken is what I want; his IBS can't reach me here, nor his moods.

The food arrives quickly. Waiter. Don't touch the plate, it's hot.

Tell me about you, Jane. How's life? You been scribbling away at your little verses?

I haven't the time or energy.

Well, that's sad if you ask me.

I didn't ask you, I say, but only in my mind.

My dull handbag is vibrating with an incoming call; I feel it against my foot, but you don't hear it so neither shall I. Your handbag hangs over the back of the chair, safe from the dirty floor. Maybe you chose it with a friend who said go for it, hun, it's gorgeous, a real investment piece, you'll get a load of wear out of it.

Do you like it? you say, having followed my eyes. I splashed out. Don't judge me.

I don't judge you.

We return after nine. It's too late to claim an early night, so I stay awake. You bustle, pouring port into a little glass and chattering on – they said this, and they did that. The liquid catches the fingers you use to hold the glass steady. You wipe it on your dress.

I stand watching you. I did this when you were little, wondering how you could play so boldly – you swung from climbing frames and laughed if you fell. Some people know how to bounce.

You ask about tomorrow. I say I don't mind, it's up to you – we can see how we feel. You gulp the full glass in response. Loud, clear. You smile and turn to pour some more. I used to drink port at Christmas.

I think perhaps I might like some of that, I say.

Really? Are you sure He wouldn't mind?

Sorry.

What are you apologising for?

You fill a little glass for me. I carry it into the living room and fill the Jane-wide space on the sofa. Ours is always clear but rarely used. His saggy chair is a different story. He'll have been too busy preparing fish tonight. Poor fish, hooked from the murky lake, lying across the plate next to peas, if he can find them in the depths of the freezer. And his drink of choice: cold, cold water, laced with just a splash of what-harm-could-it-do.

Port is as rich and sweet as I remember. I let it linger on my tongue.

Your beautiful blue bag lies beside me. I pick it up and inhale the leather. It has a crocodile skin pattern, with a short handle and a longer one for over the shoulder. *Mulberry* is threaded in gold, matching the circular gold clasp, singing luxury. You have worked your heart out for this, arriving at the office before everyone else, shoulders falling into your chest, back bending forwards. Yes, Cara Contradiction, you're my little star, despite all this mess. You deserve everything.

But does cleaning and slicing count for nothing?

I try it on, hanging heaven on my shoulder. The strap falls across my body and feels right. It longs for a new dress to match, untainted by age or burden, the colour of clarity, confidence, and conviction. The colour of sea, sky, and flowing ink. The colour that has been stolen from me.

You clatter in the kitchen, banging things into the bin, spritzing Dettol on the surfaces. Then you smile from the doorway as you remove yellow gloves. Housework complete. It's you watching me now.

Looks good, you say.

I put down your bag. Sorry.

You erase my apology with a shake of the head and sit beside me, crushing magazines and goodness-knows-what-else, your weight tilting me towards the sofa's centre. Makeup is coming away from your face.

It's lovely to see you, you say, prodding my arm with a sharp red nail, sending a little jolt.

I simply nod and squeeze your hand; words sometimes feel too painful.

Okay, random ideas for tomorrow. Manicure? New outfit? Ha, by the time this weekend's over you'll never want to go home, sorry hubby!

My words have dried up like he always wanted. Words took me away when he needed me. Needs me. Always needs me. How could you abandon me, Jane? It's only for the weekend. Right sure fine do whatever you want if that's what you want then fine. Scribble, scribble away at those little verses. Right sure fine do whatever you want if that's what you think is important then fine.

Jane, I was only teasing earlier, you know that yeah? About him. Exciting is great, sure, but it must be nice in a way to just live together and share everything and have that steadiness you know? And if you're happy I'm happy?

The 'if you're happy I'm happy' had too loud a question mark. I never wanted to risk your happiness as well as my own; for a moment it feels as though it's all slipping.

Yes, manicure, new outfit, I say, quickly, saving both of us just in time. That sounds nice.

Does it sound nice? I don't know anymore; I really don't know.

We sip our drinks and listen to Friday-night laughers in the street. I play with the idea of staying for a whole week, holding it in my hands and hanging its weight off my shoulders.

Tomorrow will be the test. Perhaps you'll pin down my hands, give me talons like yours, and slip a scarlet dress over my head. No, blue silk it must be; as blue as Neptune, sapphires, and impassioned gas flames; as blue as the leather-bound notebook under my bed that he'd shamed into an old shoe box during another last relapse.

Jane? you say.

Yes, I'm perfectly fine, answering a question you hadn't asked, and it's the truth in a way; his scorching excuses can't burn me here.

You sure?

You're trying to read my mind, coax explanations, but I can't respond; I've travelled far far away to a changing room. A single sound and the mirror walls might fall like the sides of an explosion box and leave me naked, exposed. Your shock would splatter red on my bare skin, form a purple stain on the dropped dress. Then I would tell you more about dull-old-git than you're ready to hear. Then you would really know. But today is Friday and that's a Monday revelation and I'll still be here to tell the tale.

I slide the dress up my body, avoiding the mirror. You're here with me now; you have found a way to follow silently, climbing through my teary eyes.

A whisper: Jane, are you in here?

A little louder: Jane?

Yes, I'm here.

The walls are still standing and so am I, wrapped in notebook-blue silk. You peek past the curtain, gasp, say oh my goodness how fabulous you look! Here, let me zip you up all the way. Perfect. Absolutely perfect, Jane. Wow, just look at you...

I can't yet, but you have written those words on me. I'll pretend and pretend and pretend to believe them. Until I do.

Reflections of a Mature Woman Who Took an Unfortunate Tumble

This is an uncomfortable realisation to have when you're nose deep in the ground on a coastal path in Cornwall: I have never loved anyone or anything.

The sun is about to set. I always walk at this time of day when people are on their way home to spend time with their families, to have dinner, or to while away the evening in a busy pub. I was late setting off today, hence my foolish haste, which caused me to trip over a jutting stone on the path. I landed heavily on my right hand and heard a crunching sound. My hand stings and my back hurts. I'm scared to move. Maybe if I don't move, all will be well. Maybe none of this has happened.

I don't have a mobile phone; why would I? The obvious thing to do would be to shout for help. Surely there must still be someone around. It's been a hot day and the beaches beneath me are always full of visitors. But I don't shout. I don't do anything apart from lie here, thinking, listening.

The wind swooshes through the long grass, ferns, nettles, and… all the other foliage that I should know the names for but don't. My father used to try and tell me when I was a little girl: 'This is a such-and-such, and this is a such-and-such, and smell it, Rosie, just drink in that scent!' It's a nothing. I can't remember because I didn't care. I wanted to do what I wanted to do.

All I can smell now is dirt, moist dirt, sandy dirt. What would happen if I didn't bother getting up? Would I die? I wonder how long it takes for someone to freeze to death. Who would find me? Some early-rising dog walker, I imagine. I hate mornings as much as my father loved them, and they did him no good, just reminding him how long and hard a day can be when you're unwanted – could barely look after himself, let alone me. I hate morning people; if they're energetic enough to rise early then they're energetic enough to inflict cheeriness on others.

It's autumn, and the weather is on the turn. I can feel a dampness, a coolness, a shift from the blistering day we've just had. Nose in the ground, it is becoming increasingly hard to breathe; I must turn over. I press my left hand down. My back hurts but there's no choice. My right hand is useless, and as I roll over it, it twinges. I fall hard onto my back and know that I won't be able to move again, not for a while at least.

Hello, sky. You are a scramble of blue, white, grey, and pink – a lazy salmon pink. We haven't quite reached the full sunset yet. Just a few feet away from me, the ground falls towards Carbis Bay. I can hear the waves break on the beach, just hisses really, barely louder than the breeze. Families usually huddle up in their brightly coloured windbreaks. I wonder what it's like. I've lived here all my life, moving between this-and-that jobs to fill my time, and it's never occurred to me to sit on the beach with other people, eating picnics, laughing, paddling the air with my feet as I lie on my stomach and read, or dig holes with buckets and spades that will probably be broken by tomorrow – the flimsy plastic junk you can buy down in St Ives.

I keep expecting to hear laughter rising from the bottom of the cliff, but I suppose it's too late. My eyes had been too fixed on the path ahead to notice who was there. There is something sharp under my neck – perhaps a root from one of the bushes beside me, or another stone like the one that tripped me up. I move my head a little, but it only makes it worse. The sky is becoming increasingly grey; the sun runs away to set above Porthmeor Beach.

It's getting dark. I close my eyes and imagine I am at

home and in bed. It's far too cold for my imaginings to be realistic. I am wearing a light jacket and thin trousers with trainers that were supposed to help me be steady on my feet. So much for that.

When I reopen my eyes and look up, the stars have appeared. They come and go, clouds shuffling in front of them. Stars, stargazing, such romantic things. Or so they say. I wouldn't know.

The closest I've come to romance was on a walk through a botanical garden a few days ago. I'd sat down on a bench under a something-tree – sorry, Father, I wish I had listened – to catch my breath, and a tabby cat slunk up and jumped onto my lap. I was too surprised to resist at first. Now I think of it, I shouldn't have pushed it off. Yes, it landed on its feet but maybe it was hurt in a different way. It wandered off to someone else, one of the many nearby who reached out with welcoming fingers and *pss-pss-pss*. It's only occurred to me now that the cat had chosen *me*, loved me, even if only briefly. What a strange thing!

What would it be like to lie here with another person, gazing out into the universe, sharing a romantic moment? No, I cannot imagine that. This is not romantic. I am lying in the dirt, staring out into the universe, acutely aware of how small I am, how insignificant, unloved, and disconnected from everything they say truly matters. *Twinkle, twinkle, little star, how I wonder what you* think of me. Do you mean something? Many people seem to think so, like the young woman at Tesco, the infuriatingly slow cashier, who engages in chit chat with anyone who will listen. She is always talking about star signs, constellations. Silly stuff really. What do these stars mean tonight? They mean I tripped over, couldn't get up, and now I'm in the dark. Alone.

I wake up suddenly. Oh, goodness, I'm freezing. I can barely move my fingers, and yet I'm strangely hot too.

Feverish. Something woke me. I wasn't sure what it was at first but can now feel it on my bare face and hear it pitter-pattering on my jacket. No longer able to see the stars, I close my eyes again to protect them from the raindrops. Rain, rain, rain. Before my mother decided to abandon us, she used to say that if you can't sing in the rain, you're destined to drown in it. Is that true? I try to make a sound, but my throat won't play along. I'm drowning.

The sky is light grey and hazy; it didn't manage to cry itself out overnight. Something different has woken me. There is a snuffling sound and then a golden head appears; a moist nose pushes into my cheek. I feel warm breath thawing my numb cheek.

'Oh, my goodness, are you okay?'

For a moment I think it's the dog talking. Then his owner appears.

'Hello?'

'Hello,' I reply, but it comes out all husky, phlegmy, and barely audible.

'Are you ill?'

'No.'

I'm telling the truth, but it doesn't feel like it; I'm soaked right through to my underwear, as though I've wet myself, and am amid a late-life crisis. Is that a form of illness?

'Injured? Can you move?'

I don't even *want* to move. I am more attached to the mud on this path than I've been to anything in my entire life. I've never liked being a human; I don't know how to do it. I have always felt like a floating spirit, someone whom others look through and walk through while they live their full, exciting, meaningful lives. It doesn't matter if I die.

'Can you move?' he repeats, crouching beside me and putting his hand on my arm.

'Yes,' I whisper. 'I think so.'

I open and close my hand, gently; it cannot be broken, just sprained.

'We need to get you to A&E.'

Before I know it, I am sitting, then standing, as light as air with a strong arm around my waist. The young man is rambling away, reassuringly – at least, I assume he's trying to be reassuring, but it sounds more neurotic than I'd expect from a 'cheery morning person'. There are slight hesitations as he speaks, verging on stutters. Maybe he's an early riser because he wants to avoid people as much as I do.

I don't know how he manages it, but we stumble along the path. The dog, a golden retriever, nuzzles my leg as we go and lets out a whimper. His head tilts up towards me with a questioning stare. The pain in my hand and back has been reduced to a dull, throbbing ache.

When the young man has hauled me up the uneven steps to the road above, wheezing with the effort, he sits me down on a bench that overlooks the bay, takes his phone from his pocket and dials.

Last night felt like a near-death experience. It wasn't. It was just a foolish old woman lying on a coastal path between the villages of Carbis Bay and Lelant, because she tripped, fell, and then decided not to get up – it was only later that I found I *couldn't* get up. I wanted to try out how it would make me feel to give in completely. Well, I shall tell you how I feel: I want it to matter if I die.

I want to rise early tomorrow and return to that botanical garden to ask someone who reminds me of my father, 'Would you tell me what this flower is? It smells divine.' I want to sit on that bench I was on before, the one with the cat, and open my lap, not accidentally but invitingly, and when it leaps up, put my hand on her fluffy warm back and hear her purr and not let her wander off to anyone else. She's mine; she chose me. Then when I'm done, I'll go to Tesco to buy myself a treat, not because of any exciting occasion, but just because it's Tuesday and I'm alive. Maybe I'll see the cashier, the one who says all the nonsense about stars. I'll tell her the month I was born and ask what it means. I could tell her I was stargazing last night – yes, alone, just because I felt like it, and it rained and the stars disappeared, but it was fun, so much fun, until it wasn't. I'm all right now though, so we'll laugh about it. I'll pick up my shopping bags and dash out into the downpour, because however many times you've been let down and however drenched you become, there are always reasons to sing.

Perhaps after I've done all this, I shall come back to earth and remember why I was never a plant person, cat person, star person, rain person, or singing person, and instead think about my rescuer – the wet black nose, the shaggy golden fur, the deep black eyes, the way he looked at me the whole time. And now that I know where he walks, and when, I might be able to bump into him by chance, stroke his silky ears, and tell him he's a beautiful, good boy and I can't believe I hadn't ever met him before. There was more depth to his gaze than I thought possible in any living creature. I know he understood. He struck me as someone worth getting up for.

Seven Ages of Lone

I am 80. Doctor is talking to me as if I am a child, leaning forward in his black swivel chair, the tips of his fingers joined. I rub my arthritic knees, the corduroy tingling my palms. The end must be near now.

Do you have any family, Mr Rogers? he says. You must speak to a specialist about your memory, and you need someone to go with you.

I do not answer. I do not have any problems with memory, or any family – both flow in and out of my mind, all day, every day, without fail, without compassion, without…

Mr Rogers?

I don't want to discuss this, I say. I simply need something for the pain.

He thinks I must speak to a specialist about my memory problems. I do not have any memory problems. I remember clear as anything, not that it was completely clear that day; it was like a child's painting – a sky with lonely blotches of white. Mother working on a stew, oblivious, onion seeping out of the house. Little girl moulding mud. Flashes of red poppies on the field.

Mr Rogers, this is your third appointment this week…

His face is a stormy Rembrandt, as if I am doing something wrong, tired lines creasing and un-creasing as he jabbers on. It is nice to sit here though, seeing the doctor tapping at his computer, with his flow of customers, all day, every day – customers who do not have to pay. He says I must speak to a specialist about my memory problems. I do not have any memory problems. I wish I did.

I am 69. Safe from the rising wind, I sit in front of the electric fire and television. Neither is switched on. Silence is a loyal companion.

This room will eat me in the end. Every surface is covered with books and newspapers and paintings, all piled up, waiting to fall. The unfinished canvases are my only regret. They rest against the saggy burnt-orange sofa – no, not saggy, why should I lie? The sofa is perky, unused. It merely supports my artistic failures. I could never get her face right, the dimples, the angelic twinkle, the thrown-back head. That day unravelled us all.

Someone tickles the front door. A couple of flicks of the letterbox, *tap tap*. It cannot be the postman, as he came and went this morning, letters piled up on the mat – bills and impersonal flyers – and he is one to wake the dead anyway. No, it is someone else. A visitor. My heart flutters, persuading my knees to uncurl, and I creak to the door.

No one. It must have been the wind.

I stand there a while, safe from the unfinished canvases, legs trembling in the October cold. I look out into darkness.

I am 52. Is this the answer to my prayers?

Good morning, welcome, says the fuzzy-faced man.

His grip is limper than the month-old cabbage in my refrigerator, but it is a friendly hand and the first I have shaken in a while. I pass the fiery flowers and read the news sheet: *All are welcome to His table.*

The morning sun shines through the stained-glass windows into a room full of heavy-coated people; a modern church built in an old style. It cannot decide what it wants to be – pews and play areas.

I sit at the back, sketching flowers on my sheet, hopeful daffodils waiting for their colour. We rise and fall between hymns – I feel a sense of belonging for the first time in years. *Therefore, he is able to save completely those who come to God through him, because he always lives to intercede for them.*

121

Communion.

The gowned man looks like Professor Tolkien. Up they go and kneel before him and Him. They trickle back to their pews afterwards, silent and revived. My stomach groans, crying out, yearning. I want to tear the bread and wine from his hands, toss one to the birds and drown myself in the other. And yet I cannot move.

I lower my head and flick through the bible. *When justice is done, it brings joy to the righteous but terror to evildoers.* Lord, let justice spare me.

For a moment, numbness spreads, taking away that day. But taking away that day, it takes away her. The pain seeps through me again.

The whole congregation has returned, none meeting my eye. They rise to sing their final hymn. I leave before the end and return to the fresh air, fleeing from terror and the fiery flowers. I search for daffodils.

I am 30. The green acrylic trickles down my brush. The trees are done; the church's green door remains. People pass on their way to work. An old homeless man leans against the building, dressed in shabby grey, sitting on old newspapers. He has a bundle wrapped in a dirty sheet.

My housemates were involved in a sit-in at Hornsey last night.

Come with us, William, they said.

They had barely spoken to me previously. Would I have found acceptance if I had said yes? I admire their activism and drive to help humanity, but I am better off in a park, away from judgement – contemplating and capturing.

The homeless man rises and disappears for a moment. A lonely man. I lean down and swill my paintbrush in the jar of water, squinting as I come back up, the sun rising from behind the church.

A navy suit bends down to pick up the bundle. Something boils in my stomach. Is this how they feel when they protest in our art college?

Excuse me! What are you doing with that?

Clearing the area, he says.

I throw my palette down on the grass and run towards him, heart throbbing. Those are my things! I say.

The navy suit freezes mid-bend. The homeless man hobbles back, and we stand there in a triangle of tension.

One walks off eventually, muttering, defeated. The other thanks me, takes my hand and holds it for a moment. 'You're a saint.'

Kind eyes in a worn-out face. I nearly ask his name, but the words catch in my throat, and before I know it, he's gone too, shuffling away with his precious bundle and the faint smell of urine. I will never see him again. So much for activism. So much for saintliness. Some things can never change.

I return to my canvas, remove a fly and a blade of grass from the palette, and finish the green door.

I am 17. She is beautiful. I have watched her every morning since she moved in. I make a gap between my beige bedroom curtains. She lives next door and works in the village shop, but I never talk to her. What would I say? Hello, Miss Rosalie; I just wanted to tell you how beautiful you are, with your bright blue eyes and Marilyn hair, and how much I love you.

Today, she is wearing a beige roll-neck pullover, tucked into a tight tweed skirt, which makes it difficult for her to get on her bicycle. This is the part I cannot watch without remembering that day. August 21st 1942. We raced, oblivious… My hand trembles and I allow the curtains to close, just as Mother enters.

Pull yourself together, William.

I'm trying, I say.

Yes, you are.

The lines in her forehead never leave. I did that to her; have done that to her again and again. She is further from me with every day that passes.

Will you tidy your bedsheets, at least, she says, or have some fresh air?

Or a job. That's what I hear. The best treatment for melancholia, my doctor said – leave the house, gain employment, and everything will improve. Mother did not tell him. Why would she?

That evening, I watch Rosalie return, her back curved with tiredness as she dismounts and takes her bicycle around the side of her house. Dishevelled, artificial hair. Her eyes are not bright blue – they are dull blue, like sky and cloud mixed together. Lifeless. Oblivious.

Perhaps I wouldn't have noticed her at all if it wasn't for her light hair and the similarities of their names. The R, the three syllables.

Rosalie and…

I am 10. Miss Iris spoke with Mother and Father yesterday. Father will not listen to me now.

Go, he says. Look both ways before crossing.

Father hates me. He hates that I fear school, fear the lane, fear everything. He hates me for what I did. He will always be at war.

Mother is watching from the window. I used to run the other way sometimes – not now Miss Iris has spoken with Mother and Father. I pause at the gate. Look right, look left, look right again, up the dirty hill lane. The field in front is not happy today. I shiver.

I'll go, you said, flicking your blonde hair over your

shoulder. I almost see you for a moment and then you disappear. The lane is empty.

Nobody talks to me at school. Mother says I should smile more. Father says it doesn't matter; I am there to work. I sit far from everyone in breaks, behind a tree trunk. If I talk, something might happen to them too.

You are the only one who understands. I think about you all the time, all the time. Have you forgiven me? You are my favourite. I love you.

William?

I jump up, twig snapping as my foot slams the ground. Miss Iris is all folded arms and black hair.

Who are you talking to, William?

I cannot think of a reply. Eventually, she shakes her head and walks back to the school, tottering on stubby black heels.

I do not tell Mother and Father. Miss Iris will speak with them again soon enough. I go to my bedroom as soon as it is seven o'clock and climb under the sheets. I let the tears fall. Now, only now, I dare to name you. I whisper you into my pillow.

Roberta.

We are both 4. There are white blotches in the blue sky, making the light run around us in funny ways. We are in the garden, making pies, looking up when a lorry drives past or cyclists swoop down the hill. My twin is crouched over the wet mud and keeps wiping her hands on her purple dress. Mother will be cross.

Roberta! I say.

Yes?

I poke my little fingers into the holes of her cheeks that get bigger when she smiles. She has mud on her face too now. She laughs, falls back with a bump on her bottom, and laughs more. I laugh too.

Mother is cooking in the kitchen. It smells tasty. I look towards the window to make sure she is not watching us. There are poppies on the field across the lane. I wish I could get some for Mother – then she won't be so cross about the muddy dress.

Pick them, says Roberta.

Mother told us not to go out there, I say. She'll know.

You're scared, she says, flicking her hair. Scared.

You go then, I say. I dare you.

Roberta stands, throws back her head and tries to wipe off the brown sludge before running towards the lane. I pass my little mud cake from hand to hand. She opens the gate and looks back with her angelic twinkling eyes.

I see the bicycles. I see her freeze. I hear the screech of the brakes.

Purple is flung to the ground.

My scream is silent; it will never stop.

A Little Guidance about Precious Items
Displayed Meaningfully

We suggest you start by purchasing a vase with Antique in the name, preferably the colour gold, its paint a little tattered but not too much; something appealing, though not necessarily beautiful in a way that the average person would appreciate.

Get a bouquet of fake flowers to fill your own emptiness as well as the vase's, seeing as you no longer have anyone to get them for you. (Please, no more moping about circumstances that were fully within your control.) Any colour will suffice but choose carefully because some might be seen as garish, and we wouldn't want that now, would we?

Whether the vase has been shipped over from Peru or rushed into your life by Amazon Prime, the journey may have caused a little chip on the rim. Given that it is equally ugly both ways around, we would advise you to put it chip-side to the wall. They will never know, and what they don't know won't cause you to be expelled from their good books.

Remove the label from your recent acquisition. Add it to the dusty line of pomposity on your mantelpiece, fill it with the purple silk blooms, and convince yourself it's worth more than it is. Shouldn't be too hard for someone like you.

Try to stop thinking about the chipped rim. It's considered bad form to hang on to such small concerns. Things like that drive people away: strangers, loved ones, even husbands.

We know we're right and so do you. Chip-side to the wall and move on.

And now you are ready to convince them. There is nothing like an ugly, maimed piece of art to spark conversation at your party, so make the most of it. (Is this piece new to your collection, Felicity?) Jut your hip out like a jug handle, poised to tell them all about it, and wait for them to finish telling you about their posh Shropshire holiday. Any minute now.

Compose a story of the vase's origin that will satisfy them of its importance. Justify the chip, which they're bound to notice despite your best efforts, and give it meaning: a battle scar from a life of adventure.

Encourage your guests to take the vase in their hands, push its artificial contents aside, turn it around and around, delve inside with curious fingers, feel the roughness within.

Let the idea sit with them; let it linger, undisturbed, until they reach their verdict. You may hold your breath, though it serves no purpose. Accept the verdict, whatever it is, because that is what classy people do. If they want to believe you, they will, and if you've followed our guidance to the letter, there's no reason on earth why they shouldn't.

Quite a piece, they say. Where did you acquire it? A fascinating addition, Felicity, something to treasure.

Thank them profusely. Make sure they know how much their approval means and that your other vases are all filled to the brim with it. No room for flowers, fake or otherwise. Only them.

Maintain your composure when they add, Are these meant to be roses? Really, it's difficult to tell. Spread your mouth into a convincing smile, laugh along with them, convince yourself it's not at your expense.

Keep laughing. There, perfect. Now stop.

And then, then it hits you. It hits you hard what you've become. You've netted your pretentiousness, finally. A bit late but still. Pull it from the water and let it die. Congratulations.

Now to reel in theirs. Come up with a second story. Tell them the new vase was given to you by a friend while on a luxury canal holiday in Shrewsbury. See if they go along with it. This will be the test.

Well, well, well. They have the audacity to pretend that they've been there, lived there, partied hard there, drifted between the canal's imaginary banks, stargazed, mulled over the wonders of the universe.

Smile. Smile, meaningfully. Smile, triumphantly. Watch them crack.

There is no canal in Shrewsbury.

Try to take back the vase before it slips from their canapé-greased finger, smashes on the hearth and explodes fragments, submerging the whole carpet with jagged pomposity.

If the worst should happen, the broken-ceramic tide may rise and likely will. Scramble onto a chair, a table, anything in the room that's higher than people's expectations. They'll backtrack that maybe it wasn't Shrewsbury they were thinking of and it is easy to forget and maybe they made a mistake. Oh, they did indeed.

Watch as the sea climbs their legs and their torso, until the pesky chip is on their shoulders. Amazon Prime, you should tell them, inadequately packaged, chucked onto the doorstep without a thought.

See how the purple roses bob on the surface, their thorns drifting ever closer to the horrified faces of your esteemed guests.

Then you should be all right, although we would recommend that you wait until they are fully submerged before moving from your safe place, to ensure they don't cause you any further harm.

We hope this helps. Good luck, Felicity. You're going to need it.

As She Lay in That Green Dress from M&S

'You remember this one, though, don't you, my love? Barbara Streisand. You remember, don't you? Of course you do.'

While Jacob remained kneeling beside the bed with his knees supported by a flat pillow, the carer had a hand on his hunched shoulder. In his left hand, he held the old MP3 player that one of his six grandchildren had passed down to him; it crooned painfully in the sanitised room of Trewartha Nursing Home. Jacob smoothed down the sheet that covered Barbara, who lay unconscious – his own Barbara – and then rested his hand on her warm stomach.

He turned to the young carer, who wore a black cotton face mask underneath a smudgy plastic visor, and muttered, 'I'm sorry, sweetheart, I can't wear this anymore.'

Leaning over, bringing herself closer to his hearing-aided ear, she said, 'Of course, Mr Roberts. I understand. You do whatever you need to do right now.'

'I really can't, I'm sorry.' He popped off his disposable mask and let it drop to the floor; she picked it up, folded it, and put it in the pocket of her white protective suit.

'Barbara? You know this one, don't you?'

'She does, I'm sure?' The carer glanced towards the door, as though waiting for backup or fearing that someone might burst in at any moment. 'I'm sure she does. Err, it's a lovely song.'

'Barbara Streisand. Evergreen, from *A Star is Born*. Do you know it?'

'Mr Roberts, you—'

'Our wedding song. She loves it, always dances, even tries to sing.' A smile crept onto his tired mouth, his tone lightening. 'Tries.'

'Oh,' said the carer, looking puzzled. 'Not a good singer, then?'

131

'Sweetheart… I'm sorry, I don't know your name.'

'Sophie.'

'Sophie.' He shook her hand, lingering for a moment to glance at her crinkled latex gloves and his own crinkled bare hands. 'It is lovely to meet you, Sophie.'

'You too.'

'Well, I suppose we have already met. Anyway, Sophie, what was I saying?'

'Your wife wasn't a good singer?'

'Sweetheart.' Jacob spoke with deliberation, as though trying to explain a complicated equation to a maths student of less-than-average intelligence, something he'd had to do many times over the years. 'My lovely wife – still so lovely, is she not? – my lovely wife is the worst singer I have ever heard in my whole long life. Yes, a very long life. How old would you say? Guess, Sarah.'

'Sophie.'

'My apologies, Sophie. How old do I look?'

'Oh, um…' She frowned. 'Um.'

'Eighty-eight. Four score years and eight. Or five score years minus twelve. Yes, I prefer it that way, don't you? It sounds ancient, perhaps, but distinguished.'

At that moment, another carer knocked gently and entered before either of them could respond. 'You okay, Soph?' he whispered. He was a gangly young man who'd had to bend his head to get into the room.

Sophie nodded, silent, and readjusted her face mask.

'Can I have a word?'

She stood, slowly, her knees crackling, and left the room with him; Jacob barely seemed to notice.

'Yes, you enjoy singing, don't you, my love,' he said, patting her hand.

Barbara lay on her back with her eyes closed. Her arms were both straight, stretched out over the white sheets, pinning them like a paperclip. Jacob ran his hand up and down the arm on his side, squeezing gently every now and then. He studied her face. There was a map of wrinkles across her sunken cheeks and flakes of dead skin that had dropped from her brow onto her pale, almost translucent, eyelashes.

Sophie crept back in, this time remaining by the door, and Jacob grunted with the effort to turn and speak to her. 'Sarah, would it be possible for you to make my wife a cup of tea? I am sorry to bother you, but she hasn't had anything to drink for quite a while and her lips look dry.'

'Mr Roberts…'

'Coffee would suffice, if the tea here is… Well, I am afraid she is a little fussy when it comes to tea. I remember once when we were on a train from London to Glasgow to visit our eldest grandson at university – studying mathematics, I'm pleased to say, and he graduated with First-class honours… What was I saying?'

She didn't reply but returned to his side.

'Ah, yes, the train. My wife took a sip from the cardboard cup, nudged me, and said, "Darling, is this tea or coffee? I really can't tell!" We laughed and laughed. I really can't tell, she said! She was always like that. We met when we were sixteen years old, in school. I'm afraid I tied her pigtails to the seat rail on the school bus, and yet, fool that I am, instantly regretted it and she caught me trying to untie them. I expected the verbal lashing I deserved and was shocked when she simply laughed and pushed my shoulder away, not roughly but playfully, and that was when I knew she had an excellent sense of humour as well as beautiful red hair – *Anne of Green Gables*-esque, one might say – and I still see her like that even though all these years have…' His voice faded. 'Barbara? I… Barbara.'

133

'They're here,' said Sophie, gently. 'Mr Roberts. Jacob?'

She could have told him sooner; they had arrived a short while ago, but she stalled them. He needed more time, and needed Sophie too, needed her gloved hand on his shoulder as he looked down at his wife in her green dress. It was Emerald in the 90s when they picked it up in a Marks and Spencer January sale; faded to something like a mossy shade in the early 2000s; and now, it was more like her eyes, the colour they would have been if they hadn't fallen shut.

He looked up at Sophie, confused; it was as though he'd never seen her before or couldn't remember how conversations were meant to work.

'Excuse me, sweetheart, what did you say?'

She looked down at the scuffed carpet.

Jacob suddenly grabbed his wife's hand again, gripped it hard; had he not noticed before? The skin whitening, her body growing cold, the devastating words spoken in his ear as Barbara's face drained...

'I'm afraid she's gone,' said Sophie. 'I'm so sorry.'

Jacob shook his head, frantically pressing the MP3 buttons, moving it from track to track and playing only a second of each, until he found the right song.

'You remember this one, though, don't you, my love? Barbara Streisand. You remember, don't you? Of course you do.'

Dark figures entered, in solemn respect, accompanied by one of Jacob's daughters and the grandson who had graduated from Glasgow University with First-class honours. They began to well up as they saw Barbara – Mum, Grandma – lying there, so still.

'Oh,' whispered Jacob. 'Yes. Yes, I understand now.'

Sophie reached underneath her visor and pinged the

black mask off, revealing chapped lips, a worn expression, and the trails in her makeup from seeping eyes.

'I'm sorry for your loss, Jacob,' said Sophie, placing her hand on his shoulder once more. 'So sorry. Can I... make you a cup of tea?'

Dear Margaret, Love Fred

Margaret,
Perhaps you might have noticed that I've put out your recycling bins this morning. I wasn't sure if you had intended to and forgotten, or whether, due to their being only half full, you had judged it best to save them until next week. If the latter, my apologies.
Kind regards,
Fred.

Margaret,
You might be interested to know that I intend to hire a skip soon, too big to be filled by myself alone. You are welcome to make use of it. Anything from fallen trees to broken fridges, or even old planks from the patio.
Kind regards,
Fred.

Margaret,
A belated happy birthday. It is a shame that you could not have a proper celebration. The balloon display is most impressive, though.
Best wishes,
Fred.
P.S. I find it hard to believe that you have reached the age of 70. I am happy to report that, health allowing, it is a wonderful decade. (I say this with some trepidation; I have three years more before I can give a comprehensive account.)

Margaret,
Thank you for your note. It was much appreciated.

I'm glad you liked it. A happy coincidence: I also love hedgehogs. I'm sorry that it wasn't a birthday card; I thought it best not to venture to the Post Office in this 'present climate', seeing as I am in the 'vulnerable' category. (As are you, now, I might add!)

I suppose I have always been this way. I cannot think of the right things to say in person. My mother once said that I could be a great orator, if my mind were to work a mere five seconds quicker; it is no longer a problem with close family and friends, but I still find it difficult with relative strangers.

Best wishes,
Fred.

Margaret,

Thank you for your note. It is rather fun, isn't it? It puts me in mind of a young lady I once knew; we used to enjoy exchanging secret letters. She also lived next door. It is not often that the concept of 'history repeating itself' feels so optimistic.

Best wishes,
Fred.

P.S. For the sake of full disclosure, I must add that my association with the young lady ended when she 'took a shine' to the postman. I trust that will not happen in this case!

Margaret,

Thank you for your note. I can't quite read your second paragraph, but perhaps you could tell me what it contains in person.

That would be delightful. Should we pretend to bump into each other, coincidentally? Should we walk on opposite sides of the road? I am, of course, joking. I shall meet you outside at 'precisely 10am or thereabouts', as my dad used to say.

Best wishes,
Fred.

Margaret,

Thank you, again, for a lovely day. It was most enjoyable, although your knowledge of sea birds puts me to shame. Perhaps we might take a different route next time, somewhere with hedgerows, for instance. I would fare much better.

Love,
Fred.
P.S. When we next meet, would you mind if I walk in front? My hearing is not what it was, and two metres is quite a stretch.

They Didn't See Him

And that was how he came to be stuck in the paddling pool, legs up over the rubbery turquoise side, head barely above water. It was quite a strain for his poor neck, but given what was at stake, he was prepared to make the effort. No one likes to drown. As garden parties go, this was a rather pleasant one – proved, if proof be needed, by the response to his plight. They turned the music down in consideration, if it could be called music, and came to help the old man. It reminded him of the birth of his sister, where women had encircled his mother – she was splayed out and whimpering like a cat trapped out in the cold. He'd sneaked in to see what was happening, unnoticed, pushed cruelly into second place. In this instance, he was the encircled one – although, it was more like a water birth. It was an odd thing to be thinking while lying flat on his back. Parents rushed up, no doubt fearing the strange man with a sudden smile on his face. They had to grab their children from the pool because of course the little devils didn't mind the waves they made. Others gathered around, eyes wide, and strong young men were suddenly motivated to heroism by the young women with their summer frocks and glasses of champagne. Sleeves were rolled, attempts were made. Firstly, they simply grabbed him by the arms and heaved. He cried out in pain. His back. They retreated and regrouped, stroking their un-bearded chins, probably wondering how it had happened in the first place. It was difficult to say whose fault it was. A man had stepped back into him and caused him to fall, yes, but had he been unwise to stand so close? His sixty-seven years seemed to have taught him very little about that sort of thing, when it came down to it. Nothing at all in fact. How close should one stand to another person? Secondly, a rolling technique. It was a good idea in theory, though in practice he was a large man and didn't take kindly to being treated like a beached whale. He claimed more back pain. He had been large since he was a young boy and was always told he should eat less. He had thought of that. He had even thought of that at this garden party, before the unfortunate incident took place, but it is difficult, when most kindly invited to a neighbour's event, to decline offers of cheese heaped on crackers and tangy crisps and cream-covered strawberries. Thirdly, he found a solution by himself. He turned onto his front, on all fours, managed to get a foot beneath him, and was then assisted to a standing position by more aspiring heroes, although this time they were heroines, with scant regard for their dresses. A few onlookers clapped. The whole thing was deeply embarrassing. Thank you, thank you, he said, gripping the top of his water-weighted beige trousers – the ankle region was pale, but the darkness slowly trickled down. Everyone was attentive to him, despite not knowing who he was. His lower back had long since stopped hurting, apart from the occasional twinge, which was no worse than usual. They kept asking though, most kindly, and he placed the back of his hand on the region. Still rather sore, he said. They tilted their heads and offered him glasses of champagne, to help him through the ordeal. It was nice to be a person. Carl John Rogers: the man who was stuck in a paddling pool.

Three Pairs of Bed Socks and Two Hot Water Bottles

'How was Christmas?'

'Your Uncle Steve was happy enough.'

'Brandy?'

'Gallons.'

'Bless him. What about you?'

'The worst yet, I'm afraid. I received three pairs of bed socks and two hot water bottles. Tea?'

'Ouch. Yes, please.'

'Ouch is an understatement. How old do these people think I am? Honestly… Are you still taking all that sugar?'

'Yes, please.'

'Do it yourself, I can't watch. So, I've made a decision.'

'Oh?'

'It's so nice to see someone young for a change.'

'Young, eh? Thanks.'

'All relative. Anyway, it's nice to see you.'

'Sorry, it's been a while. Work…'

'I know, I understand. The thing is, I'm sick of old people. They never do anything but grumble about their aches and pains and their neighbours and their families and the state of the world. Honestly, it's driving me crazy. And they try to drag me into their misery… and give me old-lady presents.'

'Mum got three different lavender giftsets this year. She hates lavender, always has. You're both victims of old-lady stereotyping.'

'Your mother's five years younger than me. It's no laughing matter.'

'Sorry.'

'It's all right.'

'When you start getting coffin catalogues through the door, you can really panic!'

'That's it: from now on, I'm going to become youthful again. You know, like in that film, the one where the man ages backwards. I'm going to do it.'

'Sounds good.'

'I'm serious, darling. I need some life in my social life. Where do all the young people gather these days?'

'I wouldn't know. I'm an old person in everything but age. I hang out with books and things.'

'Benjamin Button. Ages backwards in that film.'

'Never seen it.'

'Neither have I.'

'What's wrong?'

'Nothing's wrong, darling.'

'Then why are you phoning me?'

'I thought you would like an update. Wouldn't you like an update?'

'On the aging backwards thing?'

'Yes.'

'I'd love an update.'

'CrossFit.'

'Excuse me?'

'CrossFit. I saw a poster at the library. It's a gym thing, says it's open to all ages and abilities.'

'Please tell me it's April 1st…'

'Nowhere near. Don't be silly, darling. I've looked it up on the internet, and I have to say, it looks like a good deal of fun. It is a high-intensity workout regime, involving a huge variety of exercises, such as gymnastics and weightlifting.'

'That sounds dangerous. What about your hip?'

'What about it? It's the old one that gave me grief.'

'It might be worth running it past your doctor.'

'She won't mind. She's always preaching at me to keep active.'

'She meant getting up to make a cuppa and taking gentle walks, not becoming a bodybuilder.'

'I'm too lazy to become a bodybuilder.'

'All ages, indeed. It's like when organisations say, "We're a friendly and welcoming group" – it never is. It'll be a snooty group of teenagers in neon Lycra. Trust me.'

'I thought you wanted me to age backwards. I thought you wanted me to push myself out of my comfort zone, to develop new skills, to become a New Me, even if it is a little late for New Year.'

'When did I ever say that?'

'You're family. It's implicit, isn't it?'

'I love you. You know that. You're an inspirational human. Please don't join CrossFit.'

'I love you too. Maybe we can meet up next week? Bye for now.'

'Auntie… Auntie?'

'Hey. Iona, isn't it? I'm Tony. How's it going?'

'Well, we haven't started yet.'

'Ha, good one.'

'Nice to meet you.'

'You too. Excuse my hands, bit sweaty. Pull-ups.'

'Goodness, is that blood?'

'I've stopped using gloves.'

'Goodness.'

'Don't worry, love, you'll be fine. We take it slow. Work on form. Build up gradually. Boom.'

'Boom, yes, that's good, yes.'

'So, fundamentals. It's important that you understand these basic movements before we throw you into a class – gets a bit mad. Let's start with squats. Here, sit down on this box, as you normally would.'

'All right.'

'Right… Oh, okay, we might have some work to do.'

'Did I do it wrong?'

'There's no wrong, love. We're all about optimising movement, building technique and strength.'

'Have I been sitting down incorrectly all my life?'

'Gather round, everyone. Right, single-unders to warm up and then I want you to work on your double-unders.'

'Excuse me, Tony, could you explain what double-unders are, please?'

'Yeah, sorry, love. Rope goes under twice for each jump. Don't worry about them. Do singles. Can you skip?'

'Yes, I used to do it all the time when I was a little girl.'

'Boom.'

'That was a while ago though.'

'Once learnt, never forgotten, eh? Riding a bike. Right, come on, get moving people. Simon, shift back a bit – your barbell's in the way. Wow, Iona, what on earth did you do to that rope?'

'I'm sorry.'

'That's more Tangled than the movie.'

'Sorry?'

'You know, Disney? My kid is always… never mind. Karen, you do box steps – reduces impact on your knees.'

'Yes, coach.'

'Core tight, Ben. Don't arch your back.'

'Sorry.'

'Don't be sorry; keep your core tight. You okay, Iona?'

'I think so.'

'Good. Right, so, the workout will be a hundred double-unders – or however you've scaled the movements – a hundred air squats, and finish with a hundred double-unders. For time. Got it?'

'Excuse me, Tony, but is an air squat a normal squat?'

'Yeah, it is. Don't do a hundred. Stop after 10mins, wherever you've got up to. Watch your form, as we discussed last week – back straight, head up, keep your thighs aligned with your feet etc… You'll be fine, love.'

'I think this rope might be a little long.'

'It is. Go get another, they're hanging on the door.'

'All right.'

'Watch out!'

Auntie, what on earth happened to you?'

'Hello. Get yourself a cuppa, and a cake, if you like.'

'Auntie.'

'Don't fuss.'

'I told you not to do it. Now look at the state of you.'

'This is why we have two.'

'You could have made sure it was your left.'

'Ha. Your Uncle Steve can wash his own dishes and fill in his hospital forms and make me cuppas for a change. I tell you, darling, this is the way to go. He'll never let me out again though.'

'Crap.'

'Language.'

'Sorry.'

'Does it hurt?'

'The painkillers work a treat. The cast is frustrating though; can't move much. At least it's not twinging anymore.'

'Can I sign it?'

'If you must. Would you like half of my iced bun? I had one before you arrived.'

'Auntie.'

'Well, I'm running out of time. Don't take the cherry.'

'Can you sue or anything? I'm sure they're not meant to injure you on your first workout.'

'And I'm sure it's my responsibility to look where I'm going. I was moving too quickly. Excuse me, hello? Please could we have a pot of tea over here? Thank you.'

'You need locking up.'

'Jail or old people's home?'

'Jail.'

'I think you're right.'

'Always.'

'I'm sorry, darling, but five teaspoons is ridiculous. You're going to die young or give yourself diabetes.

'Says you, Auntie Two Buns.'

'Well, I can't stick to my principles all the time. Where's the fun in that? Honestly, darling, that's hot syrup; I don't know how it doesn't make you vomit. You ought to join CrossFit and learn what health and fitness mean.'

'I think I've already seen...'

'Oh, stop it, darling. I told you, it was all my fault. A man was practising his deadlifts – don't look so shocked, I'm fully versed in CrossFit terminology now – I tripped on his barbell. I forgot for a moment that I wasn't thirty-five, and that's all there is to it. It can happen to anyone. Well, not you, obviously, you are thirty-five.'

'Thirty-six.'

'Oh, of course, sorry. Remind me to do a bank transfer. Did you have a nice one?'

'Not bad, thanks, went out for cocktails with Darren and one of our friends. Pretty quiet apart from that.'

'Good, good, well enjoy it while you're young. Goodness knows the aging backwards thing is harder. I've decided not to bother. I'm old. That's fine. I've made my peace. It's difficult to be young when you're aching in muscles you never knew you had, when you can't even watch where you're walking, and when half the class are young enough to be your grandchildren.'

'You the oldest?'

'No. Marie pipped me to the post. She's ancient. I want to be like her when I grow up, if I survive that long. It seems CrossFit is off the cards for the foreseeable. You know what I need?'

'Feet up and Uncle Steve's tipple?'

'Don't.'

'Bed socks and hot water bottle?'

'Stop it.'

'What, then?'

'An activity that only involves my legs. Have you heard of kick boxing? I should imagine that's a possibility.'

'Auntie.'

'Or perhaps I could still attend CrossFit but only do squats and lunges and suchlike, although I should imagine I'd still need my arms for balance.'

'You're joking, right?'

'No, no, I'm quite serious. I might be old, but I'm not dead.'

'Auntie, no offence; you're actually mad.'

'Thank you, darling. I've made my peace with that too. It's what keeps me going.'

That Organ is Mine

I wake in an unfamiliar room. It might be a hospital or a prison or a similar establishment; sparse and cold. The reason I am here, as well as the precise location, is unclear at present. The ceiling is white, but of course most ceilings are. It has grey lines in places; it is impossible to tell from the low horizontal position in which I find myself whether they are the result of spiders' webs or cracking plaster. If the latter, it must be seen to as soon as possible. If Helena were still alive, casting her sharp eyes around this building, I would rectify it myself, immediately.

Across the room, there is a beige leather chair. I have a similar piece of furniture at home, accompanied by a beige stool. This chair has a stool too. Attempting to rise, I discover that I am wrapped in something, a blue and white floral material that pins me down. A twist of the head, the only achievable movement, enables me to see grey cushions propped against the wall. How peculiar! As I turn my head the other way, I see that the rest of the room is not sparse and cold, but cluttered and 'lived in', as Helena would say, if Helena were still alive.

Alongside the leather chair, there is a chest of drawers. It appears to be made from oak. Someone has made the unwise decision to place a mug on top of it without a coaster, risking a water mark. If I were able, I would remove it, as the chest is far too fine a piece of workmanship to be treated with such disregard. I should know; my own was very similar.

It was one of my first creations after we married. Woodworking was the antidote to long days of teaching, putting my hands to use, perfecting each angle, panel, joint and finish. Helena would often perch on my workbench, talking and laughing. I tried, on many occasions, to teach her the names of the tools, so that she could make herself useful and pass them to me, but she still often passed the wrong ones. I never told her. After an hour or so, she would push her body weight onto her hands, slowly, carefully, in case a wood splinter attached itself to her bottom and ripped her skirt. She would then leap off the worktop, disappear for a few minutes, and return carrying a wobbling tray, with tea in a practical pot, a plate of crumbling biscuits that she called 'melting moments' – I would defy anyone to produce finer biscuits – and a vase of large daisies from our tiny garden. I cut the oak with a handsaw while she told me about the new hymn she was required to learn for the following Sunday, the problematic key signature and large intervals; she had a small handspan.

The Methodist Church organ devoured her in width and height, but when I first saw her up there, she seemed to dominate the building. She was a beautiful woman. Perhaps not classically beautiful, but beautiful, nonetheless. Her hair brushed her shoulders, straight, dark, almost black. When she turned her head to glance at the preacher, I would study her profile; the small nose that tilted a little to the left, the pale translucency of her cheeks, the lines starting to form around her mouth even at the age of twenty, evidence of nearly continuous smiling. Remarkable.

At the end of each service, I lingered. My eyes took a real interest in the organ until she closed her hymn books and exited the church, at which point it suddenly lost a great deal of its appeal. I would return home accompanied by the feeling that I had forgotten something important.

One Sunday, she caught me looking. I walked over, trailing my hands along the tops of the pews to keep me balanced, smiled, and said hello. I asked her about the mechanics of the instrument (of which she knew surprisingly little), whether she had started on piano, how long she had been playing in church, whether she played other kinds of music, and how much she enjoyed it. She listened, patiently, answering each question with a crinkled brow. Eventually, she reached out her hand, and said, 'I'm Helena, thanks for asking.'

I was a foolish young man. With burning cheeks, I laughed and she laughed and I stuttered when I told her my name, as if I had never said it before, which made her laugh even more. Through that single, foolish exchange, we bonded.

We had a swift courtship, an inexpensive wedding, and purchased a small cottage outside Truro; it had a spacious garden shed to accommodate my workshop. She spent most of her time in the garden and the kitchen, where she ran a tight ship, but in the evenings, she was there beside me. She was a beautiful woman. I suspect the reason it took me so long to construct that first chest of drawers was not so much my inexperience or my attention to detail, but rather due to her distractions, her deliberate attempts to lure me from my task: picking up the tools I asked for and hiding them behind her, hopping onto the worktop and shuffling closer, hitching her skirt until it was far above her knees, singing 'Amazing Grace' with mock solemnity and professionalism, raising her voice the more I winced, her smile eventually breaking through the act. Her distractions were largely successful, of course. She was a beautiful woman.

Once I had finished the chest of drawers, I moved on to a wardrobe. It was a superb piece of craftmanship, if it is not too conceited to say so, made with as much love as technical skill. I worked happily to provide for my wife and the baby she carried, snatching moments to finish their unique wardrobe, usually late at night. That wardrobe meant a lot to us.

She visited my workshop less frequently, expanding in her pale pink silk nightdress. She berated me for not coming back to the house, saying I would wear myself out, that I would strain my eyes if I worked with so little light, that she would have to go to bed if I didn't stop soon. Dear Helena, constantly concerned for me. There was always another task though, something that I couldn't bear to leave unfinished, and I continued longer than was sensible. It was worth it though. That wardrobe meant a lot to us; a place to store the baby's things. It was unwise for me to take it apart without asking, especially so soon afterwards. I know that now.

My eyes move past the chest of drawers, past the fireplace, and settle on a small organ. It is not at all dissimilar to my own. I have a peculiar, unidentifiable feeling. There are magazines and books on top of the organ cover, suggesting that it has not been played in a long time. She did not return to church after it happened, she never played the huge pipe organ again. I failed to facilitate her return to music. That is my main regret in all of this. The two keyboards, the pedals, the woodwork… It looked perfect, but it was never playable. I did not fail through lack of effort. The long evenings turned into nights as I learnt what I needed to know, studying library books in insufficient lighting, considering different woods and designs. I knew I must create something wonderful, something which could not fail to please her, before I lost her completely.

This was when I made the mistake with the wardrobe. That is my main regret in all of this. Her chest heaved as she walked in and saw the parts covering the workshop floor.

I explained, of course I did: 'Helena, darling, I'm doing this for you, making something beautiful, you'll see!'

She was unreachable. 'How could you do this, how could you do this, how could you do this?'

Sometimes I found her sitting in her armchair, rocking gently, tears falling, looking at the gap in the room, the patch of carpet with an outline of where the heavy wardrobe used to be, not even looking up when I entered. Unreachable. I stopped reaching eventually. It became something she had to deal with alone. That is my main regret in all of this. The sun often rose before I realised the time and broke from my craft, broke from constructing the small organ, which...

That organ is mine. I am in my own house. It is laughable that I did not realise sooner. I turn my head back and attempt to lift it, but it is heavily balanced on my neck, sore from the awkward positioning of two plump pillows. It is a sofa rather than a bed, which explains the grey cushions. The duvet curls around me, making it difficult to move at present. I have taken to sleeping here, as it is closer to my comfortable leather chair than my bed, and the carer made it up for me properly on one of her routine visits. Once I have fully come round, I will attempt to escape from the duvet and proceed with my work on the organ.

That organ is mine. A photo stands precariously on the mess I have allowed to form; a distant figure, a haze of a purple gown and a small tilting nose on a face decorated with laughter lines. Where is Helena? She must have gone to the shop. She will be home presently, no doubt carrying ingredients with which to make a soup or stew or roast dinner; she always managed to cook a superb roast.

I am wearied by these joyful musings and the more discomforting recollections. Despite everything that has happened over the years and though I have sometimes been foolish and made incorrect judgements, I must not give up, not now, not ever. I close my eyes and see the straight, dark, almost black hair of a young lady who sits on a hard wooden bench, preparing to play the opening hymn. I see a foolish young man who holds a songbook and cannot focus on the words. I see...

I reopen my eyes and observe the cracked-plaster

ceiling, with its strange, winding patterns. Life has not been so bad, not in the end, even if it did not bring us all we might have wished. Perhaps she would have never started her baking business had our course run smoothly, a venture that took every inch of her skill and focus, of which she has much. I believe her to be, for the most part, contented. Our bond, though often strained, will never break. And there is one thing I may still be able to provide.

It is the evening. The sun is setting and the room swiftly becoming darker. It is peculiar that Helena has not yet returned. She is scared to be out alone at night, and besides, the shop must have closed by now. I wonder if she is all right. I exhale slowly, a loud noise in the silent room. I should rest my eyes for a little while longer. That organ is mine. I shall start working on it again, as soon as I possibly can, and not give up until it is playable. It will bring her much joy.

The Word Has It

Transforming.

That's it. I am transforming.

Quite a long word. It carries so much hope. A big weight for any word.

The foundation is on, my face prepared. Now then, should it be eyeshadow before mascara? Maybe I won't do any eyeshadow, just in case. 1975 it was, the risk that blighted my wedding photos.

The eye palette returns to the pink Estee Lauder makeup bag. My granddaughter would tell me to ditch mascara too, because it's gross. Apparently, it's not right to spit in a block anymore – germs, germs, germs. She tried to get me to buy a tube once, but even they expire. Right, a little concealer, a hint of blush, and a dab of old rosy lipstick.

My hair is as grey as donkeys, and I'm never changing that, not even for him. I shouldn't wipe away the years, the highs, the lows, the boring days that now seem sparkly. Even transforming has its limits: the grey hair stays, the mint tea stays, and podgy pug Mervin stays. Goodness, that sounds slightly shallow – I should have said my good heart, steely core, and fiery passion for justice. Since David died, these have remained and increased; I mean the good heart, steely core, and fiery passion for justice. Although, having said that, the mint tea consumption is getting out of hand and I wouldn't like to discuss Mervin's rotundity...

I know I'm moving a little off topic now, as usual, but how much thought can really be put into lip lining? Charles will see the change in me, couldn't fail to, and that's what he'll say when he opens the door: What a transformation! He will look down, blushing slightly, nose lost in the red carnations he brought because he's a listener and he knows they're my favourite. David listened too, especially when I became so quiet that he could almost hear the clock's ticking and the vehement thoughts whirring in my head. I don't remember David buying me flowers though, and I don't know for sure that Charles will – it's just the way he nodded when I said. I wonder if I'm boring to like such a basic bloom, but I can't help it, and I'd rather be happy with carnations than any other flower. Charles reassured me on that count, saying that they were a joyful choice, and all the lovelier for being inexpensive and lasting for a good long while.

This afternoon, he arrives a little before our agreed time of two-thirty and that's fine with me because I've been standing in the hallway for ten minutes already. It seems I've been thrown back a few decades, with a quivering stomach and the other strange symptoms of first love, even though we three were friends for years. I'm certain David would have approved of all this, just as I'm certain he's looking down and smiling, relishing our happiness and waiting to see where these developments might lead. Charles looks down, blushing slightly, nose lost in the red carnations he brought because he knows they're my favourite, and I lean forward to wrap my arms around his shaking shoulders. I'm glad I ditched the purple eyeshadow – it wouldn't have scared Charles, just as it didn't scare David, although that says more about them as men than it does about the eyeshadow. You look beautiful, he says, and he passes me the flowers, wrapped in clear plastic with the price still attached and clearly visible to me; we both know their cost and their worth. There are white ones mixed in with them, which is perfect because those are the ones he prefers, as he told me the other day; I like a man who has a favourite carnation. Poised on the bristly brown doormat, cheeks burning with new youth, I've become a basic bloom; happy, inexpensive, I've lasted a good long while, and intend to last a good while longer: transforming and transformed.

Golden Hair

Six children in high-viz jackets visited the care home. A young woman and two men held their hands, and a carer ushered them into the conservatory. It was a hot Saturday afternoon. Sun shone through the glass roof and landed on two old men who were seated there. Other residents tottered in, assisted by sticks, walkers, or supportive arms.

An old lady was wheeled in by a nurse, in a big armchair. She was a small, hunched body, a burgundy cardigan, and a fluff of short grey hair which curled over the twisted collar of her white blouse.

The three girls and three boys clustered around a linen bag, picking out of it brightly coloured percussion instruments. There was an attempt to manoeuvre the children into a straight line. The young woman quickly counted to four and they began to sing, 'Old MacDonald Had a Farm', accompanied by maracas, rattled in a chaos of rhythm.

The old lady's face stirred, as though she recognised something and strained to remember what it was. The young woman handed her a blue plastic tambourine. The old lady laid it on her grey-skirted lap, running her fingers around the small metal discs. She began to tap along – at the right speed but a little behind the pulse of the music.

Most of the children had gentle, lyrical voices, but one of the boys was loud. He became fidgety after the fifth song, seeming to have no wonder in twinkling little stars and what they are, and no patience to pretend. A fidget chain began. The adults exchanged looks, released the boys and girls from the untidy line, and asked if they could please put their instruments back in the bag more gently, please. The fidget-instigator rubbed his mess of hair and looked at the old lady in the big armchair.

'And what is your name, my lovely?' she asked, taking him by the hand.

'Tim.'

'You have a lovely voice, Tim.'

He rocked back and forth, heel to toe, balanced by her grip.

'Such lovely hair,' she said. 'It's golden, isn't it.'

'Ginger,' said Tim.

'Lovely golden hair.'

'Mummy says red.'

'The light,' she said. 'Such a lovely voice. I had a lovely voice. Well, it's been a while.'

Leaning forward, she touched the boy's hair, finger curling loosely around a lock. Tim stared, as though trying to work out what she was.

'Such a lovely voice.'

'Right, I think it's time we made a move,' said one of the men.

Tim adjusted his high-viz jacket and allowed his hand to be taken by the one who had led him in.

'My name is Amelia,' said the woman. 'Such a lovely voice, Tom.'

Tim's eyes didn't leave her until he had stepped over the conservatory threshold and into the dark living room. The old woman's hand remained suspended for a moment before coming to rest on the peeling faux-leather arm of her big armchair. The tambourine slipped from her lap.

I Resolve to Die at Sixty-five

December 31st – 07:00

It is my final day of being sixty-five and the final day of my life.

It was my fortieth birthday, Dec 31st, 1995, when I jotted down the words: *I Resolve to Die at Sixty-five*. That journal is open beside me. I did not express why I had made the decision, as it was not something I would forget, and it seemed crude to put it into words; her illness was too raw. How does one come to terms with their mother's sudden deterioration? One can only try to avoid the same fate.

I do not know how my death will come to pass. 'Come to pass', an intriguing expression with a biblical quality. 'Come to pass away' is better still; it is less exact than 'I do not know how I will die' but involves a delightful play on words. I am not sure how I will come to pass away.

I have not determined the time of my death either. This, coupled with the above paragraph, is a thorn in my side, a barbed wire in my side, a knife to my heart, a bunch of stinging nettles dragged across my bare stomach. I must clarify that my stomach is not, at present, bare – simply that it would have to be bare for the analogy to work. Upon reflection, the thorn-in-my-side metaphor is, although an overused expression, the most accurate in this instance.

The years have 'gone in a flash'. What an ugly phrase. There is something in the sentiment, however. The years line my walls – blue journals for the first five and a half, and green journals for the rest, due to a misguided decision by WHSmith.

It is time for my 07:15 coffee. I shall have it with four lumps of sugar instead of three, seeing as it is my deathday.

11:00

I do not know how to recount the morning. It started in a normal way, when I read the weather forecast and stepped out into the porch to see whether the world agreed with the BBC. It did, for once: sunny intervals and a moderate breeze. Happy deathday, Gordon.

However, I soon received confirmation that I ought not to let my life extend beyond sixty-five years. The breeze turned immoderate. That was the first thing the woman said, though not in those words – she did not seem the sort of person to use the word 'immoderate.' Her attire suggested shopwork of some kind. I do not mean this in a disparaging way.

What matter? The clock. Too much thinking; too little writing.

I must be resolute.

15:00

The day is fast diminishing. My to-do list is insignificant, but I am still at a loss regarding the time and method of my death – the only activity in CAPITALS. Activity. I'm not sure that is the right expression; it reeks of clay pottery and juvenile ball games.

Perhaps the decades will drown me, bury me, smash my head to smithereens. Perhaps it could happen naturally, or someone could be persuaded to come here and fight me, causing the bookcase to fall, like in... that novel. Oh, Gordon, which novel? It will come to me. All that comes to me now is her next words.

'Warm out, isn't it?'

I am no expert in the field of temperature, but I believed it to be no more than six degrees Celsius, a calculation that was confirmed by the thermometer as soon as I returned home. I hardly consider this to be warm, especially when combined

160

with an immoderate breeze. Perhaps she had meant it was warm for the season, or that, due to her heavy coat with a furry lining in the hood, it seemed warmer than it was.

It is only now I realise she was probably joking. It seems in keeping with her charming, jovial persona. It has been a long time since someone has attempted to engage with me humorously, and I must say, it was rather agreeable.

19:00

I have been obsessing over the bookcase death, and the name of its victim. I believe it starts with B. Something B. Which book though? Come on, Gordon, you can do better than this. I must never surrender to Google. I have no doubts about that woman and her use of Google, Facebook, and whatever else is currently poisoning mankind. She had her phone in her hand the whole time she was at the bus stop, flicking her thumbs up and down. It didn't stop her talking though. The conservation gradually comes back to me.

'Where are you off to?'

Did she want to know the location or the purpose of my excursion?

'Coffee.'

She nodded, more thumb flicking, and then a smile. 'You meeting someone?'

'I am not.'

It seems an odd thing to ask a person. It implies that they are not complete unless they are in the presence of another party – an implication I believe to be both incorrect and insulting. However, I chose not to contradict her.

'Have you made any New Year's resolutions?' she asked.

I hesitated momentarily.

'I haven't,' she continued. 'It's best to just live your life, isn't it?'

'Certainly,' I said.

I must cease these foolish recollections and make dinner now. As it is Tuesday, I should be eating spaghetti bolognaise for my last supper, but I have a craving for baked beans on toast, and I'm in the mood to indulge myself.

23:00 (Late – 23:22)

Most pleasant aspect of the day: a nice woman spoke to me, under no obligation.

Most unpleasant aspect of the day: forgetting which book included the bookcase death.

Observation of the day: pain can be more intense as an onlooker.

Mother had barely seemed to notice her sixty-six-year-old mind becoming more like a ninety-year-old's, but it impacted me greatly. However, I have no children to grieve for me. So, if I do not notice my own deterioration, what does it matter?

I consider this further, accompanied by my 23:15 hot chocolate. A glance at the clock had informed me that it was already 23:17, but given recent developments, I went ahead with the journal session and hot chocolate anyway.

Mother used to tell me I was far too obsessed with schedules and finer details – I expect the lady today would view things similarly. Controlling, inflexible, Mother would say. I do not agree. I like things to be in order, yes. Life is chaotic and confusing; who would not want to simplify it as much as possible? It is why I favour books. They hint at life's complexities whilst containing them within neat, tidy blocks. (Oh, which had the bookcase death? I shall probably remember as I am trying to sleep.)

It is strange to write with my drink beside me. I look up occasionally and touch the side of the mug with my fingertips, to ascertain the temperature, as I should not like it to become cold. You may be surprised that, despite the allotted time having long since passed, I am in no rush to finish writing in my journal – not as surprised as I.

I doubt she keeps a journal; she is the sort of free spirit who would prefer to go out with friends, swinging her wavy red hair, even at that stage of life. I should guess forty, the same age I was when I decided, or a year or two above. The area around her eyes wrinkled when she smiled, which was often, but when it fell to a neutral position the skin was somewhat smooth. Although it is unlikely that we shall meet again, I would like to know who she is. I believe her badge said 'Abigail' – aside from the Yellow Pages, my ability to find her is somewhat limited. This, admittedly, is one of the few benefits of websites such as Facebook.

My last statement is evidence that I should be in bed, asleep, safe from these strangely pleasant, warm thoughts. There are other things I would like to communicate, and it is a source of frustration to me that, despite these sensations being some of the strongest I've experienced in a long time, I am struggling to put them into words. They are like vivid dreams that fade when you wake and leave only feelings. Perhaps this is what it means when people describe themselves as 'only human': willing to forsake reason sometimes and not overanalyse their emotions.

23:59

As Abigail said, 'It's best to just live your life.'
I shall never again make a resolution.

January 1st – 03:22

Howard's End by EM Forster! The tragic death of Leonard Bast. Upon reflection, it would be an extremely unpleasant way to go.

To Live

The station is as bleak as my smashed-up flowerbeds. A cold gust of wind nearly sends me flying into the platform.

I have a big decision to make today, dear – perhaps you could help? No, it'll be too late by the time you get back to me, unless it's by divine intervention, of course. Too late. Just like this train, which is just as well because she's always late too. Here I am tapping my foot, metaphorically speaking – at my age it would be unwise to even lift my toes off the floor if unnecessary – and she's probably just leaving her house.

I'll pick you up on the way, Gwen, I told her in Week Two, and we're on Six now. No, no, I'll get a taxi, she said – values her independence she does. I'd value her being on time… but that's none of your business, Noel Stockley, none of your business.

Ah! Her grey coat billows, hood flipping on and off as she hangs onto the rail, dragging herself up the ramp. I would go and help, but unnecessary movement. And she values her independence. Did I mention that? Perhaps I'd feel the same if I were her, coming from ten years of shuffling behind her husband's wheelchair. Not how it was with you, my girl.

Two years this weekend, spritely to the end, smiling the winces away. The Big C. No, call it cancer, Noel, cancer – it's no prettier being euphemism-ed. Euphemised, dear, euphemised. Too like euthanised, you said. Well, we could give that a go, I said, and you chuckled till it hurt and then were silent for a good while.

Come on, Gwen, there you go, easy does it. She grasps this week's project, with its gaudy pink cover that would shock even a young girl. I nearly started it, maybe read it a while back, who knows? But, you see, the lawn needed help and my knees were too disgruntled afterwards. Despite the arthritis, you might see me on my knees again when it's time for *Ulysses* – God, save me from Week Nine! After all, I'm nearer to the grave than the… the… womb? Cradle? I don't know.

'What a gale, eh?'

Gwen cups her ear. 'Pardon?'

'I said, it's very windy!'

She shakes her head and says something else. Too quiet.

'What did you say?'

'Pardon? I can't hear you, Noel,' she all but yells. 'This terrible wind!'

Nearly said 'pardon' back, just for fun, you know? We'd be pardoning all day, around in circles, then she'd give me shut-up-Noel eyes, no doubt. I never knew shut-up-Noel eyes could be so beautiful.

'Never mind,' I say, as the train appears.

Doors hiss. The people surge, pushing on before the others are off. Hardly a brain between them.

She gives me her hand now, for a moment, and I feel the extra weight in my knee-joints as she pulls herself up the step. Could have chosen the handle, but no. Independent, my foot! What is that on her hand? Interesting. Right, Noel, mind the gap, please mind the gap.

'So, you did it, then?'

'Yes.' She holds up her left hand.

A table between us, Bangor disappears. I stretch out my legs into the aisle, folding my arms across my stomach. She is slumped back, shoulders forward, embracing the stupid curve of the seat – sit up girl, you would tell her. The ring overtakes her finger. Plain. Gold. Big.

'Was it difficult?'

'I had thought about it for a long time.'

'I meant for the jewellers.'

'Ah. I've no idea.'

You'd like that about her. Strangely blasé, even when distressed, as she clearly is. Her eyes are weepy. Hang on, my vision's a blur too. Damn the Welsh wind!

'I don't expect so.' She moves her hand back to her lap, her body rocking a little in motion with the train. 'They're professionals. They checked I was sure, of course, and I signed forms.'

'Ah.'

'What will you do? Have you decided yet?'

Your rings are still in the jewellery box. Where else? I removed them before they could slip off your skinny finger. First time I'd thought about it, when Gwen told me her plan – melt down, reform. How strange! Gloriously commemorative or damned sentimental? What do you think?

'No. I don't know. Why did you choose now?'

'Ten years on Wednesday.'

Ah! She did tell me last week. In one ear and out the other. Well done, Noel. 'I'm sorry.'

'It's not your fault.' A whisker of a smile.

That smile. White teeth. If I squint, or if my eyesight worsens, they wouldn't be unlike yours. Great set of teeth, the first thing I noticed – on her, I mean. Your wild hair grabbed me first. Hers may have been wild once, but now it's too short to tell.

'It seemed appropriate.' The teeth disappear. 'As I say, I've been thinking of it for a while now, and it's a way that he can... you know...'

'Be with you.'

She nods. 'You know what it feels like, don't you? To have that person sharing every adventure, every big moment. Gone. But now...' She raises her hand again, examining the rehashed jewellery. 'I can take him with me, wherever I go.'

166

Her finger is bound to his, by a circle of gold. I'm somehow bound to her too – bound by cancer. His end and yours. There, are you proud of me? Cancer. Cancer. Cancer.

Gwen's silent now, as am I. The landscape is tearing by, the window splattered with rain that I didn't realise had started. Empty feeling in my stomach – yes, yes, I know, I should have had breakfast. Ah! I know that rumble of small wheels.

'Crisps, please, salt and vinegar. Anything for you, Gwen?'

A hesitation instead of her usual, 'No, thank you.'

'Well, perhaps…' Her forehead creases. 'Perhaps I could have some of those biscuits.'

'Really?' Now we're really getting somewhere. Independence be damned. 'Of course. Biscuits too, please.'

'I can pay.'

I hand over the money before her gold-ringed finger has reached her bag. She's lefthanded. Never noticed before. Crisps in my right, I open the packet with my left, flashing the thin gold ring – we couldn't afford more than that, could we? Not for mine anyway. I'm glad of it. Don't even know I'm wearing it, or at least I didn't. Now it's all I see.

Maybe it's time to take it off. To melt, or not to melt, that is the bloody question. Maybe I should move it to the other hand, like some people do, instead of melting them all down and wearing them forever. Forever, pah! A couple of years more like – this creaky ol' man won't last much longer! It's good to hear you laughing.

Gwen turns back from the window. 'What are you smiling at?'

You are laughing, aren't you? Such a lovely laugh.

The train jolts out of Colwyn Bay. Our table is carnage. Empty green bag of Walkers, Viennese biscuit packet with accompanying crumbs, dirty tissues, and sandwiches. The sandwiches were an afterthought – I caught the trolley on its way back. Cheese and onion. I know, I know, what a party at 11am! Feeling a little sick now, if I'm honest. Ate too quickly and you know I don't have much of a travel belly, even on stiller days – just as well I can glimpse out front when the train takes a bend.

'Don't like this.' Gwen turns, craning her head to see where we're going. She grips her bag with both hands, scrunching the leather. 'Never travelled in such a storm.'

Distract her, Noel, distract her. The pink book sits on the table, between biscuits and my empty sandwich box – a safe distance from stickiness, don't worry, dear.

'Have you read it?' Course she has.

'Yes. Have you?'

I shake my head.

Tut. 'Why ever not?'

'I'm Noel, I haven't read it.'

'You did last week.'

'That's because I had nothing better to do.' I pick a piece of lettuce off my navy trousers.

'How can you say that?' Her eyes have come alive. Lovely.

'Easily.'

A gust buffets the train. You're not telling me what you think, not helping me with my decision. Please don't go quiet on me, dear.

Gwen leans forward. 'This book club fosters the appreciation of masterpieces. How can you make them sound like a last resort?'

'It was sunny. I wanted to be in the garden.'

'Well, we've had our sun now. It's probably going to rain for the next few weeks.'

'No, it won't.'

'Why did you even sign up?'

'For fun. I still have a train ride to Chester, the delightful debates, the enjoyment of being in the room with such enthused literary souls. Is that not enough?'

'I don't understand you.'

Yes, she does. Her sparkling eyes understand me. What a delight to argue!

'Well.' She crosses her arms. 'You could have read it in the garden. There!'

'What's the point in burying your head in a book when you can look up at the glories of nature?'

Something's wrong. I don't know what, but something's wrong. Two of the train staff are behind the glass door, gesturing frantically.

'Yes, but if you sign up to a course, surely it's your duty to follow its rules.'

'I'm too old to force myself to do things I don't want to do. Why should I?'

'Yes, but if…'

The train takes a bend, and then I see. A flash of orange clothes.

They can't hear the screeching brakes. They can't hear the horn that makes Gwen cover her ears and shrink into her chair. They can't hear the shouts from further up our carriage. Workmen on the track.

'Bloody hell!'

They finally hear, finally see, and jump out the way. All but one.

'Noel?'

Something has caught – his clothes, or his foot! Don't look, Gwen, please don't look.

She turns. 'Oh my God, oh my God!'

Our food packets jolt off the table. I close my eyes.

Too late.

Death comes for all of us in the end.

Those were your exact words, weren't they? But it

keeps missing me – on and on, round and round, life spins. Not for him. Did you see it happen? Ask the guy upstairs, the question we want to ask, all of us: *Why?*

The boy in orange, killed for keeping our tracks safe, killed because of the loud wind, killed because I'm so damned resilient to death.

The wind knocks our carriage some more as we sit tight. Waiting. We felt nothing, nothing at all. But the train can't just carry on like nothing's happened.

'Are you all right?' I say.

Gwen huddles into her grey coat, faced away, barely nodding. I can see more of her face in the window reflection. You and your smiles. You and she are so different now. Gone are the teeth. A ghost, with tears streaming. Waiting.

The train powers up again, groaning into motion, slow.

We will soon be arriving at Flint. Please make sure you have all your personal belongings and please take care while leaving the train. Thank you.

Automation.

She looks up. 'I need to get off.'

'Shall I come too?'

Nothing.

I follow her, along with others, none of us talking. A little girl is crying. She didn't see, of course not, but she knows. Daddy burying her head in his chest and saying 'It's okay, it's okay' reeks of disaster. She knows. She can feel it. Even her runny nose can feel it.

Reckon we'll be stopped a while. The air hits us hard and I'm glad.

In the end, without us, the train did just carry on like nothing had happened. It had to. We can't, dear, that's for sure.

I let out old air from my lungs. Onion. 'Gwen.'

She's not facing me, has to turn. 'Yes?'

Lord, what a mess. 'What are you going to do?'

'I can't go.'

What's that now? A strange pulsing in my stomach. 'I understand.'

'I feel... sick.'

Gwen looks even older now, poor girl. You'd know what to do, wouldn't you? Shall I wrap my arm around her? No, perhaps not. Perhaps, but, then again...

My gold-ringed hand grazes her sleeve, just briefly. 'Do you need to sit?'

Gwen nods and practically leads me to a bench, sinking into it like an old woman who's back in her favourite armchair. I sat in yours the other day. Felt nice, your bottom carved it out nicely. Dear Cassandra. You'd know what to do. You'd know what I should do too, slap me round the head with it more than likely. I know you.

And you know I've decided.

'Gwen.' Her name sounds nice through my lips. Ha, don't worry, I'm not about to start singing it. Still me.

She hasn't heard.

'Gwen? Would you like to get a cup of tea... or coffee?' I don't know which she has, after all these weeks! 'Somewhere in town. While you get your strength back.'

She draws a small mirror out of her bag, recoils at the reflection and quickly puts it back. Her hands are shaking. 'Thank you, Noel, but... I need to go home.'

I stand and offer my hand. 'Of course.'

'No, no, I'd rather be alone. You go.' She gets up. 'I don't want to ruin your day.'

'You aren't. I'll come with you.'

'No, no. Thank you.' Gwen touches my arm and begins to walk towards the bridge.

I nearly follow her. I catch sight of railway crew, carrying something, and quickly turn away. Too late.

A young man tries to help me up the step, bloody cheek! Barely a toenail in the grave, me. I sit down in a half-empty carriage, alone this time, although you are with me. You'll always be with me, won't you, dear?

As the train accelerates, Gwen walks along the station with her little shuffling footsteps towards the arrivals and departures board, clutching that pink book. She could stride now if she wanted, I'm sure, but no. Her striding days are over. Mine are too, but I'll sure as hell try, for as long as I've got legs.

The bloodied trouser swung as they carried away his leg. Did that boy use to stride? Do you know? Is he there with you now? *Why?*

No, no. You may be silent, but I know what you'd say.

The weather's calming down. Back gardens flash by, all green and happy, not bashed about at all from what I can see. By the time we reach our destination, we'll be out of it, I reckon. Blue skies, warm sun – Chester will be glorious! And then what?

Bloody hell, my joints are about to explode, bloody arthritic old man! How did I miss that a minute ago? You're laughing again.

I put my feet up on the empty chair opposite, to get the blood flowing. Swollen fingers too. Now's the time, dear, it's starting to pinch. I pull, wriggle, and pull again until it comes off, leaving a white line all round my finger. Life goes on, Noel.

If the World Were Ending

The smoke starts to seep into the room and the unbearable heat makes my skin shrivel and crackle. We wrap our arms around our munchkins, who say nothing, do nothing. Their faces are much more serene than you'd imagine, but then why should they be scared when we're not? You catch my eye and reach over to hold my hand. We say a prayer.

Outside the apartment, flames tear through our city; their roar becomes louder by the second. Inside, we are surrounded by the flaking yellow walls that we never got around to repainting. You mentioned it early this morning, Mr Fix It, which is funny now. Dishes have piled up too, unsoaked, unwashed; I'm glad I didn't waste time doing them, because what does it matter now the world is ending?

Our lives together flash through my mind, right back to when we met. It was the golf club meal, our two churches joining to celebrate Christmas on two different tables. Together but not together. We were the Young People, bringing the average age down by decades, and had kept attending despite everyone else falling away. The Old People's voices rumbled with doom and gloom. Their time was nearly over, but we were nineteen and wouldn't let it consume us, choosing contentment rather than fear of what we would lose. Dissenters.

It was love at first sight – for you, not for me. I liked you, respected you, knew we would have a good life together. That's all. Perhaps that's what true love is anyway, not tingles and flutters, or the feeling you'd be dead without them. I thought that was what I wanted, but I also knew if I let you go, life wouldn't be as full as it could have been.

You've lined the doors with clothes, wettened with toilet water; we gave the clean water to our munchkins to ease their thirst, or at least stop their tongues sticking to the roof of their mouths, as mine is now. None of us has talked for a while. What on earth do you say at a time like this? I love you. It's all going to be okay. We didn't start the fire. Ha! Billy Joel. No, we may not have started the fire but it's about to eat us. A distant education reminds me, *Don't use the lift, dial 999, walk don't run, the smoke will kill you before the flames...* Oh, and, *Drop and roll, drop and roll,* if you go up in flames – not that rolling would extinguish the end of the world. But this strange smoke hasn't strangled us and the fire is yet to appear. Maybe He's giving us a moment longer, to reflect and prepare.

As the weeks and months had passed, something shifted. It started the day you unblocked my toilet. I stood in the doorway, all trussed up in my red duffle coat and the high ankle boots I tottered along in, ready for a Saturday-night date at our favourite restaurant. I was still at the stage of doing everything I could think of to impress you, however unnecessary that was; I wore makeup and everything. When you arrived to pick me up, I told you about the toilet situation, and you immediately removed your shiny black shoes – without untying them – and bustled into the bathroom. You took off your suit jacket, thrust it at me, and asked for the plunger. I knew we would be late for our reservation, but it didn't matter; there was a feeling spreading up from my stomach and into my chest. Tingles and flutters. Right there, at that moment, as I buried my nose into your jacket.

The grey cloud comes closer, wraps itself around us, and shrinks our bubble. It's getting hard to breathe. Little hands tighten inside mine. Fingernails dig into my palms. Kerensa Grace and Olivia Jane – two for the price of one, beautiful, dark, full of nine-year-old energy. They look like you today, faces crinkled, as though trying to solve a problem. Our Little Miss Fix Its. But this one is out of everyone's control. There's peace in that.

You smile at me, the man who has protected me, respected me, adored me fiercely, as though our vows were tattooed on your forehead. It's no less intense now. And I know you're happy that the toilet is in good working order for the end of the world. That's just the way you are.

I smile back and wink at you; a tear falls with it. Sitting here, waiting for our New Life, something strange and unknown, I'm glad I took this risk. I chose my man and had children with him, knowing The End couldn't be far off, and we've had longer than expected. I thank God for that each day. I wouldn't have had it any oth—

Credits

'A Long Line of Plastic Straws' was longlisted in the Bedford International Writing Competition 2021, won the Faversham Literary Festival Competition 2022, and was first published on Faversham Literary Festival's website.

'Naughty Step' received Highly Commended in the Anansi Archive Flash Fiction Award Autumn 2021 and was included in their anthology, *The Nine Lives of Billy Nightjar*.

'Clara By Every Name' was longlisted in the Exeter Writers Short Story Competition 2022, longlisted in the Brick Lane Short Story Prize 2022, and first published in the anthology, *Brick Lane Book Shop: New Short Stories* 2022.

'dashed' was first published by CaféLit in August 2023 and included in their anthology, *The Best of CaféLit 13*.

'Right Now' received Highly Commended in the Crossing the Tees Book Festival Short Story Competition 2020 and was included in *Crossing the Tees: The Fourth Short Story Anthology*.

'Becoming Lavender' was first published by Potato Soup Journal in May 2022.

'Unspoken, Unheard' was first published by CaféLit in December 2019 and included in their anthology, *The Best of CaféLit 9*.

'Those Nice Suits' was included in Bridge House Publishing's 2020 anthology, *Mulling It Over*.

'**Kiss My Stretchmarks and Call Me Tiger**' was first published by Every Day Fiction.

'**When the Tour Guide Still Smiles**' was awarded Second Prize in the Cranked Anvil Press Short Story Competition January 2022.

'**Native**' was first published by CaféLit in December 2019.

'**Wayne's Name**' was shortlisted in the Henshaw Short Story Competition June 2019, shortlisted in the Bedford International Writing Competition 2019 and first published in their anthology.

'**Chanel No.5 on a Musty Woollen Coat**' was first published by Potato Soup Journal and included in their anthology, *Potato Soup Journal: Best of 2022*.

'**When Seagulls**' was longlisted in the Fish Publishing Short Story Prize 2020/2021.

'**Burning Me, Maybe**' was first published on my blog, *Hannah Retallick: I Have an Idea*, in May 2023.

'**She Went There for the Weekend**' was longlisted in the Fish Publishing Short Story Prize 2022, awarded Second Prize in the Leicester Writes Short Story Prize 2023, and was first published in *Leicester Writes Short Story Prize Anthology 2023*.

'**Reflections of a Mature Woman Who Took an Unfortunate Tumble**' was shortlisted in the ChipLitFest Short Story Competition 2022, shortlisted in the Henshaw Short Story Competition March 2022, and longlisted in the Retreat West Short Story Prize 2022.

'**Seven Ages of Lone**' won the Gwyl Ysgrifennu Ynys Môn/Anglesey Writing Festival Competition 2022 and was first published on their website.

'**As She Lay in That Green Dress from M&S**' was chosen for Bridge House Publishing's 2022 anthology, *Evergreen*.

'**Dear Margaret, Love Fred**' was first published by CaféLit in June 2020.

'**They Didn't See Him**' was first published by CaféLit in July 2022.

'**Three Pairs of Bed Socks and Two Hot Water Bottles**' was first published by CaféLit in December 2020 and included in their anthology, *The Best of CaféLit 10*.

'**That Organ is Mine**' was first published by Secret Attic in October 2022.

'**The Word Has It**' is one of the winning entries from the 2019 Waterloo Festival Writing Competition and first published in the anthology, *Transformations*.

'**Golden Hair**' was first published by CaféLit in September 2020 and included in their anthology, *The Best of CaféLit 10*.

'**I Resolve to Die at Sixty-five**' was chosen for Bridge House Publishing's 2021 anthology, *Resolutions*.

'**To Live**' was shortlisted in the 2018 Cambridge Short Story Prize and first published in their anthology, *Make a Wish, Keep the Wish Secret*.

'If the World Were Ending' was first published by Potato Soup Journal and included in their anthology, *Potato Soup Journal: Best of 2021*.

About the Author

Hannah Retallick is from Anglesey, North Wales. She was home educated, along with her two brothers. Hannah enjoyed writing creatively when she was younger, self-publishing a book at eleven years old about her grandad's cat. She often chose to voice animal characters, inspired by A.A Milne and Beatrix Potter, because at that age she didn't feel she knew enough about human nature to do people justice!

Hannah focused on music during her teen years and early twenties, playing trombone and piano, singing, and belonging to several bands and orchestras. She taught one-to-one for ten years and conducted her local junior brass bands for six years.

Following A Levels, Hannah studied with the Open University, graduating with a First-class honours degree, BA in Humanities with Creative Writing and Music, and a Distinction in her Creative Writing MA, specialising in short fiction. Her dissertation stories were inspired by the year she spent in Cornwall.

In 2018, Hannah started sending out stories regularly. She has been published in paperbacks, in e-books, and online, and has been placed/shortlisted in numerous international competitions. She was Highly Commended in the Bridport Flash Fiction Prize 2022 and won the £2000 Edinburgh Award for Flash Fiction 2024 – the biggest flash prize in the UK.

Hannah works as a writer, freelance editor, and PA. Something Very Human is her debut short story collection.

Like to Read More Work Like This?

Then sign up to our mailing list and download our free collection of short stories, *Magnetism*. Sign up now to receive this free e-book and also to find out about all of our new publications and offers.

Sign up here:
   http://eepurl.com/gbpdVz

Please Leave a Review

Reviews are so important to writers. Please take the time to review this book. A couple of lines is fine.

Reviews help the book to become more visible to buyers. Retailers will promote books with multiple reviews.

This in turn helps us to sell more books... And then we can afford to publish more books like this one.

Leaving a review is very easy.

Go to https://amzn.to/3ZuJeP5, scroll down the left-hand side of the Amazon page and click on the 'Write a customer review' button.

Other Publications by Bridge House

The Story Weaver
by Sally Zigmond

Story-telling has often been associated with weaving and
spinning. All is craft, cleverness and magic.

Here indeed we have a colourful mix of beautifully crafted
stories. Some are sad and others bring us hope. There are
tensions in relationships, fear of the unknown coupled with
surprising empathy, and accidents of birth. Death wishes are
reversed, sometimes but not always, and so are lives in other
realties. People's stories intersect as they wait for a bus. An old
cello causes havoc. A church clock always strikes twice… or
does it? Match-making goes wrong until it goes right. And so
much more.

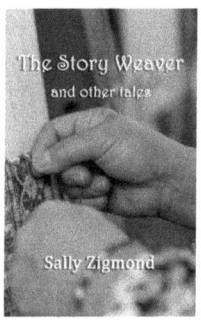

"A wonderful collection of interesting tales. A real mixture
that will delight all readers." *(Amazon)*

Order from Amazon:

Paperback: ISBN 978-1-914199-54-7
eBook: ISBN 978-1-914199-55-4

The Adventures of Iris and Zach
by I.L. Green

Iris and Zach have an uneasy but intriguing run.

A vast patchwork landscape of life is displayed through stories relating both the wonder and absurdity we all recognize. With a focus on mental health, these stories take the reader from incarceration to freedom, fear to comfort. There are celebrations of life and poetic lows. The Yin and Yang aspects of life are recognized in new and deliberate examples that instil thoughtfulness and occasionally a smile.

Order from Amazon:

Paperback: ISBN 978-1-914199-34-9
eBook: ISBN 978-1-914199-35-6

A Gentle Nudge
by Mason Bushell

Stories to soothe your soul.

In a world drowning in negativity and dark events, we all need a little light and hope. With a little adventure, romance and even music, these short stories will give your hopes and dreams a nudge as they draw a smile.

A Gentle Nudge by Mason Bushell wraps you in calm.

Order from Amazon:

Paperback: ISBN 978-1-914199-42-4
eBook: ISBN 978-1-914199-43-1